LIVING
WITH
DEATH

CAROLYN DALE

Living With Death
Carolyn Dale

CARRICK
PUBLISHING

Copyright Carolyn Dale 2015

Carrick Publishing
Print Edition 2015
ISBN 13: 978-1-77242-012-8
Cover Design by Sara Carrick

Dedication

To Linda, Jack and Beryl

Acknowledgements

Thanks to my sister Ruth, with her usual help on my manuscripts, and to editor Holly Bennett for her useful criticism. Thanks to Stacy Rose and Shelby Vevers, insurance adjusters for their information on insurance claims. Thanks also to medical ethicist, Margaret Somerville, and to forensic psychologist, Richard Walter, whose works I have mentioned in this novel.

Carolyn Dale is a pen name of
mystery author Anne Barton.

www.annebartonmysteries.ca
www.mysterycarolyndale.ca

CHAPTER ONE

"So the law to allow euthanasia finally passed," the hospital administrator remarked. "I think we had better activate the euthanasia protocol the committee drew up."

The chief of the medical staff wandered restlessly over to the window and gazed out over the complex of hospital buildings. "Yes, it passed. I don't think people have seriously considered all the consequences."

"You're right. I wonder how long it will be before the first lawsuit will be filed."

The professor of anesthesiology at the medical school was a firm opponent of euthanasia. He told his class, "You who are planning to be anesthesiologists are going to be the ones who are asked to do the dirty work. Now that you have been licensed to kill, you need to have a serious soul-searching session. You need to decide whether you are comfortable with being allowed to play God."

A gymnast who had made a mistake in a dismount and had landed on the back of his neck, resulting in his becoming a quadriplegic, heaved a sigh of relief on hearing that the euthanasia bill had passed. Finally he had a way to get out of this prison his body now represented.

Another young man, with the confidence of youth, was oblivious to the raging debate over the euthanasia law. That was something old people worried about.

Cruising along the highway, Brian Wall felt on top of the world. It was really nice of his stepfather to give him this motorcycle as a graduation present. Brian had recently received his degree in electrical engineering and was being groomed to eventually take over the company when his stepfather, Charles Packard, stepped down from Packard Electronics. Brian remembered with fondness his biological father, but he couldn't have done better in the man his mother had married after the divorce.

It was a warm, sunny day, and the new bike cruised smoothly along the highway. A slower moving motor home appeared ahead, and Brian moved out slightly to see whether he could safely pass. He saw the road curve to the right and slowed while tucking in a safe distance behind the motorhome. Behind him a following pickup also slowed, but Brian caught a brief glimpse of a speeding yellow sports car. He moved over farther toward the side of the road as it looked to him as if the car would pass the pickup and might need to pull into the spot between it and the motorhome ahead.

The sports car driver ducked into the space just vacated by Brian as a truck passed in the opposite direction, then gunned his motor with a squeal of tires and veered out to pass. The rear end of the car slewed to the right and Brian seeing it coming toward him, pulled over still more. His wheels hit loose gravel; he automatically turned to get back on the solid pavement, but lost control. He felt the tires slip and the bike tip sideways, saw the pavement coming up to meet him, and landed on his shoulder. The shock of pain from a fractured collarbone was followed by the feel of skin being ripped off as he slid along the pavement. He found himself lying on his shoulder and felt the urgent need to roll over to get his weight off of it, not noticing in his reaction to the pain, that the motorcycle was spinning toward him. The rear wheel smashed into the side of his helmet, knocking him into blessed unconsciousness.

The contractor driving the pickup saw the sequence of events and braked hard to give the car and the biker more room. He saw the youth lose control when the machine hit the gravel and saw the youth's head snap sideways as the wheel of the bike hit him. Parking the pickup so that it shielded the youth lying on the highway, he pulled out his cell phone to call 911 as he ran toward the youth. The kid was still breathing, but was out cold. The contractor wondered whether he should put the kid into the recovery position, but he realized that he might have a neck injury and decided to leave him on his back.

It seemed an age before help arrived, but was actually less that ten minutes. Other motorists stopped and he ordered them to direct traffic, and prevented one overly helpful woman from wanting to take off the youth's helmet and put a cushion under his head. A police car arrived first and seeing that the contractor was knowledgeable in first aid concentrated on traffic control. An ambulance arrived a few minutes later. The paramedics applied a neck brace and rolled the kid onto a backboard before whisking him off.

The contractor answered the policeman's questions calmly but the cop noticed that the man was shaking. "Are you feeling all right, sir?" he asked.

"Yeah, I'm okay. I'll just sit in my truck and call my workers to tell them I'll be late and they can get on with the job. I'll be fine once I get something to do. I hope you catch that guy. He's a menace on the road."

"We did. He got stopped at the next town. We know him. It's not the first time!"

"Well, I hope you throw the book at him."

CHAPTER TWO

"He is going to live, isn't he? Tell me he's going to be all right." Dawn Packard held her stepbrother's hand, stroking the back of it. She sat at Brian's bedside, talking to him, urging him to wake up. The youth lay in a limp heap, his breath coming in a slow, shallow rhythm, his muscles flaccid. An IV dripped slowly. Green traces rolled across the screens of monitors.

"It is too early to say," Dr. Bentley, the head of the hospital's neurosurgery department responded in a sympathetic voice. "We just have to wait."

"But you are doing something aren't you?"

"Of course. We are supporting his physiological functions and keeping close track of his vital signs. If we see any increase in pressure inside his skull, we'll deal with it."

"He is getting better though isn't he?" This question was from Clarice Packard, Brian's mother.

"Umm. Not really. He has not been bleeding into the brain any more, and in that sense, he is not getting worse, but he has not shown any improvement either. It is early yet." That the chief neurosurgeon was talking to the family was because Charles Packard was a member of the board of directors of the foundation that raised money to buy equipment for the hospital.

"I'll be away at a conference over the weekend, but the chief resident, Dr. Schumacher, will be handling Brian's treatment, so he is in good hands."

"Come on, Dawn, you've been here a long time. You need some rest, and if there is any change, they'll let us know." The speaker was Charles Packard, who put his arm around his sixteen-year-old daughter's shoulders and tried to lead her away.

"No! I want to stay with him. What if he comes to and no one is here?"

"There are nurses here all the time. If he comes to, they'll know."

"I want to be here when he does. He needs to see a face he knows."

"Honey, it may be days or weeks."

"Charles, get that girl out of here," Clarice demanded. "Let's go home."

"Let her stay if she insists." Charles Packard sighed in resignation. "Besides, Brian's friends from his fraternity at the University will be here over the weekend to sit with him. So there will be help in a day or two. She'll be okay until then."

"If you say so. She's your responsibility, so if she gets sick from lack of sleep and eating heaven knows what, that's your problem."

They left the girl sitting by the bedside talking to her stepbrother. She crooned to the unconscious youth, trying to remember the words of his favorite songs, humming when she couldn't remember. Telling him that she loved him and reminding him of all the things he had planned to do, she pleaded with him to wake up. He showed no sign of hearing her.

Clarice had made a play for the wealthy widower, Charles Packard, hoping to latch onto his money and easy living. Packard had readily fallen into the trap. He even liked Clarice's son, which was more than she did herself. Brian, then fourteen years of age, was growing up to remind her of her ex, Keith Wall. The boy was turning out to be good looking in the quiet, charming way that had first attracted Clarice to Keith. The boy also showed the mannerisms that constantly reminded her of her ex-husband. Furthermore, Charles had taken to the boy and as the years passed, had become more involved with his education and training with the idea that Brian should eventually take over the company. Clarice found herself becoming jealous of her son. Brian, once he got his own e-mail address, started a regular correspondence with his biological father. She had been given custody of the boy, with visiting privileges given to his father. She had moved two thousand miles away, to her childhood home of Centralia, in order to make visitation more difficult, but hadn't counted on the distance-shrinking properties of social media.

Now she shuddered at the idea of Brian ending up with severe disabilities that would require constant nursing care. She wished that he had been killed outright in that accident, on the motorcycle Charles had given him, justifying this by telling herself that he would be better off dead than seriously disabled.

Martin Schumacher carried his tray to a table and sat down wearily to eat a hasty lunch. The head of the transplant service, Dr. Steve Mendel, walked over and sat opposite him. "Hi. I understand you have a brain injured patient in a deep coma."

"Yeah."

"Not likely to survive, I understand."

"Probably not. Too much damage. But you never know. Some patients do come out of it." Schumacher took a large bite of his sandwich and chewed hastily.

"But not likely."

"No. Why?"

"There are hundreds of patients waiting for donor organs. Think of all the organs, all probably in excellent condition, that we could get from that kid. Kidneys, liver, pancreas, heart and lungs, corneas."

"When he dies, you can be sure we will try to get the family to donate his organs."

"Sure. But he might be in a coma for weeks or months, or come to and remain in a chronic vegetative state. Think of what donating his organs could do now. With this new law allowing euthanasia, you could talk them into letting him go, since he's going to die anyway, and letting us take those organs. Think of all the people on waiting lists that it could help."

"I can't do that! You've got to give head injuries some time before you give up on them."

"Isn't that just wishful thinking?"

"Yeah. Probably so. We've got to keep telling the family that there's a chance, but we know it's not likely to happen."

"In the meantime half a dozen people who could have been helped will die on a waiting list. Hey! You work too damn hard. Look at you. Living on cheeseburgers. How about coming to my house and letting my wife give you a real meal. She's a superb cook."

The resident looked up and stared at the other doctor. "Are you trying to bribe me?"

"Hey. Where'd you get that idea? Can't I offer you a decent meal just as a friend? Come on over when you get off tonight, if you don't mind putting up with all the kids."

"Thanks Steve. I could do with a good dinner. My girlfriend isn't much of a cook."

"I'll see you at seven then. And think it over."

CHAPTER THREE

The Packard family met again in Brian's room several days later. Dawn, who had kept a constant vigil at her stepbrother's bedside, occasionally sleeping in a chair and making quick trips to the cafeteria for something to eat, was sitting bedside the bed with her head lying on the edge, fast asleep. Charles gently woke her, and when she sat up and rubbed her eyes, he said, "Dawn, honey, we're going to the conference room at the end of the ward to talk to the doctors. Do you want to come?"

Dawn pulled herself to her feet and stretched, replying with a grunt and a single word, "Yeah." She shuffled along behind the parents and flopped into a chair, having difficulty keeping her eyes open.

The two doctors were waiting in the conference room of the ward where Brian Wall lay, still in a deep coma. The Packard family entered. Dawn appeared drawn and tired, barely awake in fact. Her jeans and sweatshirt were rumpled, her hair uncombed. She rubbed her sleepy eyes. Clarice, on the other hand, was stylishly dressed, her hair neatly coifed, her makeup impeccable. Charles, who had come from work, removed his tie and unbuttoned the top button of his shirt. He seemed calm and contained.

The head of the transplant service started the discussion. "As you saw, Brian has not improved. He is still in a deep coma and it is very unlikely that he will ever come out of it. Even if he did, he would probably remain in a vegetative state, which is not a life for anyone. Have you thought about what we talked about? We got the impression that you were thinking of euthanasia."

"But what if he does come out of the coma and knows what's going on?" Charles asked.

"At best, there would be a long period of having to have things done for him, like a baby. He'd have to be fed and bathed and his clothes changed. He would probably be incontinent and need to wear a diaper. It is highly unlikely that he would ever be normal again."

"So you are definitely suggesting that euthanasia would be the appropriate thing to do?" Clarice asked. To herself she said, you're not going to see me waiting on him and nursing him twenty-four/seven. I'm certainly not going to change his diapers! It was bad enough when he was a baby. She hadn't wanted a baby, but Keith had insisted. Why was it that men could always get their way?

"There are hundreds of people on waiting lists for organ transplants. With a healthy young man like Brian, his organs could be used by half a dozen people who need them badly. With your permission to euthanize him his organs can be used to help other people."

"Do you agree with that?" Clarice glared at the chief neurosurgical resident.

"Regrettably, yes."

12

"Well, if both of you think so, I guess that's how it will have to be."

Dawn jerked up her head. Her lethargy vanished. "You mean you want to kill him!"

"He is for all intents and purposes dead already." The transplant surgeon said.

"He is not! You can't kill him. You can't!"

The resident shifted uncomfortably.

"You can't kill my brother. I won't let you."

"Oh, shut up," Clarice snarled. "You're too young to know what's going on. Just stay out of this. He isn't any relation to you, anyway."

"He's my brother."

"Your stepbrother."

"He's still my brother."

"Just shut up."

Charles stepped forward. "Clarice, honey, don't you think we ought to wait a while longer before making any such decision." He had assumed, when Clarice over the course of the last few days had refused to discuss the subject of euthanasia, that she was not in favor of that act, that her instincts as a mother made her unwilling to even discuss the possibility. Now, to his surprise and despair, she apparently had the exact opposite inclination.

Clarice turned on Charles and spit out, "He's not your son, so don't try to tell me what to do. Just stay out of this. And get your kid out of here." Charles stepped back a pace at this rebuke, a worried frown on his face.

Dawn jumped to her feet and raced to the door. Before anyone could react, she was streaking down the corridor to Brian's room. She threw herself onto him, shielding his body from the people who hurried in after her. She screamed, "I'm not going to let you do anything to him. I'm not going to let him die."

Someone said "Code White" and a nurse who had rushed into the room quickly left again. Soon two uniformed security officers, one of them female, entered the room and made their way to the girl who was still shielding her brother's body. "Come along, love." The two security officers gently but firmly pried her away from the boy's bed and half led, half dragged her toward the door.

"Let go of me. They're going to kill my brother."

"Come along. The doctors know what they're doing. You can't interfere with them."

"But they're going to kill him."

"Take it easy love. Just come with us."

"They're going to take all his organs out. I hope everyone who gets them dies."

Unfortunately, this remark was overheard by a reporter for a local daily who had been lurking in the hallway hoping for a chance to get into the room to photograph the comatose young man. Even better, he thought. This was the kind of thing that would make a lurid headline.

In the conference room, the female officer tried to console the distraught girl. "If the doctors are going to transplant his organs, that means he's already dead, love."

"But he isn't. He's alive, and they're going to kill him so they can take out his organs."

The officer glanced at her partner. "Go check on that." He nodded and left the room. Shortly, he returned and motioned the woman to step out into the hall.

In a low voice, he said, "She's right. He is alive and the family has agreed to euthanasia."

14

She glanced toward the weeping girl. "Oh God! Poor girl."

Charles appeared at the door. "Come on, honey. We're going home."

The security officers escorted Dawn to the nurses' station where Clarice and the two doctors were signing papers. "I hate all of you. You think I don't amount to anything because I'm young. I'm almost seventeen, and when I turn eighteen I'm going to sue every damn one of you."

After the Packard family left, the resident remarked, "You'll need another doctor to co-sign on this, you know. The hospital protocol says it has to be two staff physicians. As a resident, I can't do it."

"You know who we can get to sign it though, don't you?" Both doctors knew he was talking about a physician who had been a vigorous campaigner for the euthanasia law.

"Yeah. Our Dr. Death."

"He'll probably come and talk to you about it, though." The resident nodded.

CHAPTER FOUR

Jon Smits, a high school classmate of Dawn and her steady boyfriend, was waiting on their doorstep. As Dawn got out of the car, he went to her and enveloped her in a big hug. "I'm so sorry about Brian. You must be devastated."

"They're going to kill him and I can't do anything about it," Dawn wailed.

"I heard. It's on the radio already. The first to take advantage of the new law," Jon said in disgust. "That's really crappy. What a way to get a first! You'd think he'd accomplished something everyone who knew him could be proud of, the way they talk."

"Oh God, Jon. That means he will be in the papers forever. Every year they'll have some sort of anniversary story. We'll never be able to get away from it."

Jon tipped her chin up and kissed her gently. "If there's anything I can do for you, hey, just ask. I'll be there for you."

"Thanks Jon." She sniffed and wiped her eyes.

"If you need anything, just call me."

That evening, after a sketchy meal, Charles and Clarice were in the kitchen, finishing their coffee. Dawn, who had barely eaten, sat curled up on the couch in the darkened living room, staring into space. The phone rang.

"Can you get that, honey?" Charles called out.

Dawn uncoiled herself and ambled over to the phone. "Hullo," she said wearily.

"Hi there. You must be Dawn. Can I talk to Brian? This is his Dad."

Struck speechless, Dawn stood there. Her hand holding the phone to her ear began to shake. "Are you there?" Keith Wall queried when he didn't get an answer.

"Oh, didn't you know?"

"Know what?"

"Brian's dead."

"What!"

"They killed him. He's dead."

"Who killed him?"

"Those doctors at the hospital."

"Why was he in the hospital?"

"Didn't anyone tell you? He got run off the road on his motorcycle and crashed."

"No. No one told me. When did that happen?"

"Last Friday. He's been in a coma and they decided he wasn't going to live, but I know he would have if he had a chance. They wanted his organs to donate to other people."

There was no answer from the other end of the line. "Hullo?" Dawn said tentatively, but all she heard was a click and then the dial tone. Slowly she put down the phone.

"Who was that?" Charles asked, coming into the room and turning on the lights.

18

"Brian's Dad. He wanted to talk to Brian."

"Oh my God. Don't tell me no one told him about Brian's accident. I supposed that either Clarice or the hospital would."

Dawn merely shook her head.

"What is he going to do?"

"I don't know. He just hung up."

"Clarice had better call him back." But when told, Clarice shrugged and said, "I don't give a damn what he does. He can just go on repairing his stupid lawnmowers in that crummy little shop of his for all I care. That's all he's good for."

"But he's the boy's father."

"I don't care." She walked away and headed for the stairs. She stopped at the bottom of the staircase and turned toward her husband. "By the way, you can expect that stupid reporter who was there at the hospital to be back. He heard your daughter making some remark about hoping everyone who got Brian's organs would die. I saw him writing it down. You ought to tell your daughter to use some common sense and keep her mouth shut." With that, she ascended the stairs and could be heard slamming the door to her bedroom.

The following day, the reporter for the daily newspaper was on the Packards' doorstep by eight o'clock. The news of Dawn's comment had leaked out, and several other reporters as well as a TV truck were also on site. When Charles answered the door, knowing what his daughter had said, he was prepared to take them on.

"Look, my daughter said something in a time of great distress. It was the sort of remark anyone might make at a time like that without really meaning it. There is no need to make an issue of it. She has prepared a statement, which she will come out and read. I will not allow any questions. She is grieving, and you guys should leave her alone."

Charles went into the house and returned with his arm around Dawn's shoulders. Dawn held a paper on which she had written her statement. She started reading in a shaky voice, but became more comfortable as she read. Her voice became firm, and when she finished, she stared at the reporter who had overheard and reported her remark, spearing him with a steely gaze.

"I am sorry for the remark I made. I wasn't really thinking. I was only thinking about my brother, who was about to die. I don't even remember what I said. If I offended anybody I'm truly sorry. I hope that every person who received an organ from my brother, Brian, does well and can lead a normal and happy life. That is the only thing that is good about what happened, so I pray for everyone who received one of his organs. Thank you."

Charles then led his daughter back into the house, shutting the door against the questions being hurled by the reporters.

CHAPTER FIVE

While this was going on, Clarice got into her car, backed it out of the garage, and defied anyone who got in her way. Two crew members from the TV truck jumped off the driveway as she apparently would as soon run over them as not.

"Where are you going?" Charles had asked.

"To the insurance company where he had that stupid motorcycle insured."

As the news media packed up their equipment and prepared to leave, a taxi approached the house and stopped a short distance away. Keith Wall got out.

"You can leave me here. I'll walk the rest of the way when those guys leave," he told the taxi driver as he paid his bill. He joined a group of bystanders, and as the media left the scene and the crowd dispersed, he walked up to the front door and rang the bell. Charles answered, thinking it was another reporter and prepared to send him on his way.

"I'm Keith Wall."

The two men stared at each other as Charles readjusted his thinking. He saw a man showing a close physical resemblance to his stepson, with a day's growth of beard, a greasy sheen on his tired face, his clothes looking as if they had been slept in. Finally, he said, "Come in. Dawn told me you called last night. I guess she told you the news."

"Sort of. But I still don't know what happened. If he was hurt in an accident last Friday, why didn't anyone tell me?"

Charles noting the haggard, unshaved face, felt a rush of empathy for this man who should have been involved in the decision to allow his son's euthanasia. "I'm really sorry. We were all so concerned by Brian's accident, I guess we weren't thinking straight. I assumed that Clarice would get in touch with you, or that the hospital would."

"I want to know why he died. Dawn made it sound like the doctors didn't treat him right. He is dead, isn't he? Or is he still in the hospital?"

"He's dead. But he shouldn't be, at least not yet. He had a bad head injury and was in a coma. The doctors wanted to euthanize him and use his organs for transplant, and Clarice agreed."

"She agreed? To let her own son die?"

"Don't be too hard on her. They told us that it was very unlikely that he would live, and if he did, it wouldn't be a good life."

"And you went along with Clarice on that?"

Dawn, who had been curled up on the couch listening, sat up and came to the defense of her father. "Clarice told him to shut up; that his opinion didn't count. She told me I was too young to have an opinion. I wanted to save his life."

"Did the doctors know that you weren't Brian's father and that his real father was alive?"

"They must have known. They knew that Dawn was a stepsister. They never asked about his real father. Look, I'm terribly sorry about this. Maybe I should have spoken up more firmly," Charles said in a troubled voice.

His hands clenched, his face red, and his body taught with anger, Keith Wall exploded. "I'm going down to that damned hospital and tell them what I think of them for killing a healthy young man like Brian as if he were an old dog. They're going to pay for this!"

He moved toward the door, but Charles, who had once played linebacker on the University football team, interposed his bulk between the smaller man and the door.

"Don't do something you will regret later. Wait until you calm down, get all the facts, then get a lawyer to go with you. I'll help any way I can."

Keith Wall's face collapsed and the tears began to flow. The larger man wrapped his arms around the weeping father and hugged him to his chest until the tears stopped, then guided him to a chair.

"What you need now is rest. You can stay here. You probably shouldn't go to a hotel alone."

"Thanks." Keith wiped tears from his face. "I'm sorry I let go like that. I've been up all night. I took the red-eye and just got here. You're right about waiting until I've pulled myself together. I was about to go kill somebody myself, or at least beat the shit out of them."

Dawn dragged herself upright, walked over to where Keith Wall was sitting and rested one hip on the arm of the chair, laying her hand on his shoulder. "You can have Brian's room if you want. Or would you rather not?"

He looked up at the girl. "I'd like that. You're Dawn aren't you? Brian was always telling me about you. He really liked having a little sister."

"Well, I loved my big brother."

CHAPTER SIX

The records office clerk looked at the next woman in line and surmised that this one was going to give her trouble; the scowl, the squirming, the tapping of her shoe on the floor to indicate her impatience. The clerk, who normally would have smiled and asked what she could do for the client, formed her face into a neutral expression and waited for the woman to speak first.

"The goddamned insurance company won't believe my son is dead unless they have something on paper. They want a death certificate."

"What is your son's name?"

"I'm Mrs. Charles Packard and my son was Brian Wall."

"How do you spell his last name?"

"W A L L of course."

"There are other spellings, so I had to be sure. Is his first name spelled with an I or a Y?"

"An I," the lady snapped.

The clerk turned to her computer and typed in the name, hit "print" and retrieved the resulting document from the printer, handing it across the counter. Mrs. Packard snatched the paper and examined it, reading it from beginning to end. When she got to the section marked "Cause of Death" she spotted the word "homicide."

"What the hell! It says here that he was murdered. That's not right!" she screamed in anger.

"I only print out the form. I don't write it."

"But this is a bunch of shit."

"If you don't agree with it, you'll have to go to the coroner's office."

"Coroner, hell. I'm going to the news media."

So on TV that evening and in the morning papers, the headlines screamed, "Coroner Says Packard Heir Was Murdered."

Early the next morning, the coroner's office was besieged by reporters from all the papers, radio stations and TV outlets. The coroner's secretary met them at the door and calmly told them that there would be a ten o'clock press conference.

The coroner, a tall, stately gentleman, was also the hospital's chief pathologist. In his fifties, he was an old hand at press conferences and with giving evidence in court. He walked sedately to the podium and with a smile turned toward the battery of cameras, recorders and cell phones.

"What's this about that Wall kid being murdered," several reporters shouted at him. "We heard that's what you put on his death certificate."

"I did not say he was murdered. I stated on the form that his death was a homicide."

"That's the same thing."

The coroner's response took on a pedantic tone. He knew how easily his remarks could be misinterpreted if he did not make them very clear. "You are not correct there. Homicide means the death of one person at the hands of another. Murder is a legal concept that I have nothing to do with. Murder is only one form of homicide. There are others."

"What, for instance?"

"War. In a declared war, a soldier may legally kill the enemy.

"Self defense. A person may kill when they face a lethal threat from someone else, or to protect another person who is so threatened.

"Capital punishment, in jurisdictions where that is legal.

"Euthanasia, again in jurisdictions where it is legal."

"But the kid died from being smashed up in a motorcycle accident," a reporter called out.

"Brian Wall did not die from injuries received in the motorcycle accident. He died as a result of having his vital organs removed for transplantation. That was a homicide, a form of euthanasia, and is legal in this jurisdiction. It was not murder."

CHAPTER SEVEN

Clarice Packard came storming into the house after a second trip to the insurance agency to deliver the death certificate they had demanded.

"Of all the damned, stupid, incompetent things I ever heard of, this takes the cake. They say they won't pay the death benefit, only the cost of repairing that damned motorcycle, and there's a deductible on that. They'll only pay peanuts for it."

"Why?" Charles asked.

"Why what."

"Why won't they pay the death benefit?"

"Because that stupid coroner said Brian didn't die of his injuries. I don't know what the hell they think he died of."

"Oh. I never thought of that. But they're right, I guess. They will assume that he might have lived for at least thirty days. I think that's the cut-off date for assuming he died from his injuries."

"But he was injured in that accident on that damned motorcycle and he died. I can't see why they won't pay."

"Clarice, honey, stop and think for a minute. I know he might have died from his injuries, but he didn't really. He died from being euthanized."

"Are you telling me it's my fault? Are you?"

Charles hadn't an answer for that. He knew the answer was yes, Brian's death was her fault, but he didn't dare say so. But the subject of death benefits made him think he'd better call the life insurance company. Since Brian was being groomed to join the firm and eventually take over when Charles retired, Packard Electronics had added Brian to the roster of essential employees who were covered by insurance. Charles picked up the phone and called his insurance agent.

"We heard of the young man's death, Charles," the agent said. "Our thoughts and prayers are with you."

"Thank you."

"I imagine you want to file a claim on the company insurance for his death."

"That's correct. I understand that there was a double indemnity clause that would pay double for accidental death."

"Well, yes. But I'm not sure the company will pay anything, and even if it does it certainly will not honor the double indemnity clause."

"Why won't it pay?" Charles' voice held an argumentative tone.

"Well, you see, euthanasia is considered a form of suicide. All insurance policies state that a claim will be denied in the case of suicide."

"What?"

"Hold on though. Let me ask you a few questions. Did Brian request, or actively agree to euthanasia?"

"He did not!" Charles was angry now. "He was unconscious from a serious head injury. He never regained consciousness. He couldn't request or give consent to anything."

"You're sure of that?"

"Yes. I am. Very sure."

"Did he ever speak to anyone after his accident?"

"A witness to the accident said the wheel of the bike hit him on the side of the head and knocked him out cold."

"Well then. The company will probably pay, but not the double indemnity."

Charles slowly put down the phone. "What's the matter now?" Clarice wanted to know.

"I had no idea the can of worms euthanasia would open up."

And that was not the last of it.

When Dr. Bentley returned from his weekend trip, he waylaid Martin Schumacher as the head resident was leaving for home.

"I am told that you agreed to the authorization for euthanasia for Brian Wall. I am very upset about that. It was only a few days from his injury. That was not nearly enough time to give the boy."

"But he was going to die," Schumacher sounded defensive.

"You don't know that. Many patients are unconscious longer than that, yet make good recoveries after they do wake up. Did you consult anyone else about this?"

"Who is there to consult?"

"You should have consulted the ethics committee."

"What do they have to do with it?"

31

"They have everything to do with it. Don't tell me you don't understand that. And furthermore, if you haven't the patience to wait it out for a much longer time than you did, you aren't going to have much success as a neurosurgeon. People will be afraid to come to you, wondering if you'll let them die if they don't recover quickly."

"But think of all the patients who received his organs, who would have had to wait longer and might have died."

"There would have been other patients on the waiting list next month. His organs would not go to waste."

"But…"

"Furthermore, those are not your patients. Brian Wall was."

Schumacher slumped on the couch in the small apartment he shared with his fiancé. She scowled down at him. "What's eating you?"

"It's about that kid I okayed for euthanasia the other day."

"Look, you aren't going to go all weepy about that, are you? I don't want to live with someone who's on a perpetual guilt trip."

"It's Bentley. He tore a strip off me today for doing that."

"So what? It's legal now. What's he griping about?"

"He can kick me out."

"What? You mean not let you finish your residency?"

"Yeah."

"Look here, you'd better start making up to him if you want me to marry you. Let him know you'll do anything. If he says jump, then jump. If he says shine my shoes, shine them. I don't want to get hooked up with someone who's going to end up being a taxi driver like those foreign doctors who come here trying to get a license."

"It wouldn't amount to that. I'd still be a licensed physician. I'd have to go into family practice instead."

"Well, I don't want to be the wife of a stuffy old family doctor in some burg way out in the boonies. So you'd better get off your ass and do something about it."

CHAPTER EIGHT

After a night's rest, Keith Wall woke up in his son's room and looked around. There were sports posters on the wall, but also ones showing electrical diagrams made into kooky art forms. He'd really been serious about his career, Keith could tell. A feeling of pride welled up in him as he relived conversations with Brian and e-mails Brian had sent describing the things he was learning. A bookshelf held the youth's textbooks, as well as some other reading material. Brian had gone in for biographies of famous people in the world of physics. There were a few novels also, and Keith approved of the type of reading his son had done. Tears welled up again in the father's eyes as he realized that he would never again talk to his son about the boy's dreams and aspirations.

He turned to more mundane material, bills, receipts, information from Centralia University where Brian had been studying. There was his diploma, not yet framed, and the program for the Commencement ceremony. "Commencement!" Keith thought in disgust. That was supposed to be the start of Brian's new life. Instead it had resulted in his being given a new motorcycle by Charles Packard, and that had resulted in Brian's death. Keith fought down the resentment that welled up regarding the gift. He reasoned that it was not Packard's fault. Keith himself might have given his son a gift like that if he could have afforded it. And Packard had paid Brian's university fees.

Using Brian's computer, Keith looked up information on the hospital's administrator. He also looked through Brian's personal papers, including those in his wallet, which had been returned to the family after Brian's death. He made a plan of attack, glad now that Charles Packard had prevented him from going to confront the hospital authorities in his state of uncontrolled anger. The anger was still there, but now it would be channeled into a useful plan. He opted not to contact a lawyer. He did not want anyone cautiously trying to rein him in.

Not knowing at what time the administrator normally came to his office, he took a taxi to the hospital, arriving a little before eight a.m. He noted a parking spot labeled "Hospital Administrator," and found a seat where he could watch the spot. The man arrived around eight thirty. Keith identified him from the photo he had studied. As the man entered the lobby, Keith fell in behind him, taking the same elevator and following him out and down a corridor to the administrator's office. It was locked and the man pulled out keys to open the door. Good, Keith thought. I won't have to go past a protective secretary. He walked in behind his quarry. The administrator turned to confront the person following him and said, "My secretary comes at nine. Have a seat."

"I'm not waiting. I came to see you and I want to see you now."

"I'm busy. You'll have to wait."

"Oh no, I won't. I think you will see me now. I'm Keith Wall. I am the father of Brian Wall, who was killed by the doctors at this hospital on Saturday."

"Oh! I'm so sorry. Yes, I'll talk to you. Come in."

They entered the office, and instead of going around behind his desk, the administrator motioned Keith to a chair and took another facing him. "Now let me know what I can do for you."

"I want to know why I was not notified that my son was in the hospital and why a decision was made to end his life without consulting me."

"You are his biological father, I assume."

"I am."

"We may not have known that."

"You couldn't help but know. My former wife, who is now Mrs. Charles Packard, said in the presence of doctors and nurses, that Packard was Brian's stepfather. Furthermore, the identification in Brian's wallet listed both his mother and me as next of kin."

"The ER may not have looked in his wallet."

"They must have. He was brought in by ambulance after an accident out of town on the highway. Someone must have looked at his identification in order to call the Packards. They got the information on where to call from his ID card in his wallet."

"I am sorry. We definitely slipped up there. I also am upset by what happened. However, euthanasia is now legal here, and the authorization was made by two reputable doctors and agreed to by Mrs. Packard."

"It was pretty hasty, killing him before he had a chance to recover."

"The doctors have told me that there was no doubt that he was going to die."

"That's not what the other doctor, the neurosurgeon who was treating him, said."

"Are you sure?"

"Yes, I'm sure. He told the Packards that he would be away over the weekend, at some conference, and that some other doctor would be taking care of Brian. But he also told them that in time, he might regain consciousness. He said Brian might be disabled, but there are lots of things that can be done these days for brain injured people."

The administrator rubbed his hands down his face and sighed. "They didn't tell me that. I'm truly sorry."

"So what are you going to do about it?"

"Mr. Wall, this legislation allowing euthanasia is new. When it was being proposed by the government, I consulted with the chief of the medical staff and we struck a committee to determine how to deal with the new reality. They put forth a protocol on how a request for euthanasia would be handled. As far as I know, this protocol was followed. We do have guidelines on how to proceed when a patient, or their next of kin, acting on their behalf, requests euthanasia."

"I am Brian's next of kin. I did not authorize anyone to kill him."

"I'm afraid we slipped up there."

"And aren't you supposed to give someone a time period to reconsider? I've read up on this new law."

"That is when the patient himself requests euthanasia. It doesn't apply to family members."

"Why the hell not?"

The administrator shrugged. "If you don't agree with the law, you should contact the government about changing it."

Keith rose to his feet. "Well, you'd damn well better get your ass in gear and make some changes to your policy before someone else gets killed by mistake." He turned and strode out the door.

In the prosecutor's office, the head of the prosecution service put down the newspaper he had been reading and sighed. His thoughts were interrupted by one of his deputies bursting into the room.

"We've got him now! That rich creep who ran the Packard kid off the road is in for it. The coroner has listed the boy's death as a homicide, so we can send Mr. Fancy Pants off to prison for a long time."

"Hold your horses. It's not going to happen."

"Of course it is. That contractor guy who saw the accident will be a good witness when it goes to court. He's not going to get out of this one just because he has a lot of money. He's got a whole stack of citations for reckless driving, but this time we've got him."

"No we don't."

"Why not?"

"You haven't paid attention to the whole story."

"So what about it?"

"When the coroner declared Brian Wall's death a homicide, it wasn't because the 'rich creep' ran him off the road. It was because the family got talked into euthanasia so his organs could be donated. He didn't die from his injuries in that accident. He died from having his guts stripped out of him. So the 'rich creep,' as you call him, can't be charged with vehicular homicide. We can only get him again for reckless driving. He'll be slapped by a fine that will only be pocket change for him, and walk out of here laughing."

CHAPTER NINE

Keith Wall stopped at the same insurance company his ex-wife had been so angry about and asked the same questions. No, they told him, they would not pay out on the loss of life claim. He had not died from injuries sustained in the accident. He asked whether they would try to get payment from the insurance company of the driver who had run Brian off the road. Again the answer was no. Under normal circumstances Brian's heirs could claim loss of income, but not in this case. The other driver's insurance company was also off the hook. It seemed that there was no end to the damage the act of euthanasia could do.

He returned to the Packard house to find Dawn the only one there, in her usual spot, curled up on the couch. Her eyes were puffy and reddened. Her body slumped. Keith sat down beside her and gave her a hug. "Can I think of you as a daughter, the same way you considered Brian a brother?"

"I guess so, if you want to."

"Maybe we can help each other through our grief."

Dawn sat up straight and spat, "The only thing that will help me is to get to my eighteenth birthday and be able to sue the pants off those guys."

"That won't bring Brian back, you know."

"I know. But it'll make me feel a whole lot better."

Taken aback by the girl's reaction, Keith rose and started pacing the room. He described his trip to the hospital administrator's office and his suggestion that the hospital revamp their euthanasia rules.

"They won't do anything," the girl snarled.

"They might."

"Well, don't hold your breath."

"Look, I don't live here, so I can't do anything about the law, but you could talk to people, to your friends and classmates. You young people can get really worked up about something you think is wrong. Older people do take notice if you make enough noise."

"What could we do?"

"Talk to their parents. Strike while the iron is hot. It's in the news now, so now is the time to do something."

"What?"

"You might get people to sign a petition to rescind the law. You can't sign it because you're not old enough, but any of your classmates who are eighteen years of age could, and they could get their parents to." Keith had only said this off the top of his head, thinking of it as a way for the girl to let off some of her bottled-up anger. He had not expected a positive response.

"Yeah. I can do that. I'll start a petition drive. We do that for all kinds of things at school, but this will have to be more widespread. We'd have to set up in the mall. I wonder how to word it."

"You'll figure it out."

"Say, why don't you sue them? It'll be more than a year before I can."

"I can't do that. I don't live here and I have to get back to work."

"You could stay long enough to get a lawyer. You're staying for the funeral anyway. People would pay attention to you but they won't to me. Come on, Keith, do it."

"Look, I don't want to get involved in any lawsuit. They take a lot of time and energy, and they cost a lot of money."

"Aren't you angry about what happened to Brian?"

"Yeah, but…"

"Well, if you care about your son, you should be willing to put your money where your mouth is."

"I don't have that kind of money," Keith explained, realizing that this girl had never had to figure out where the money to do something she wanted would come from. "And I'm saving up to buy a place where I can expand. I'd like to get a franchise from one of the companies that manufacture things like lawnmowers and snowmobiles and chain saws. That kind of stuff. I'm not there yet, but I'm putting away everything I can."

Charles came home and walked into the living room, hearing only the last part of this dialogue. "What kind of business do you have Keith?" he asked.

"I own a small-engine repair shop. I started out small, in a hole-in-the-wall space, but I've steadily grown. Now I'd like to branch out into sales. I've been investigating a couple of franchise opportunities. But first I have to find a building I can buy or lease, lease probably."

"You know, that's the way my grandfather started out, back in the thirties, when radios were a novel thing. He started out with a repair shop, expanded to sales, went into television, and kept getting bigger. He had already started Packard Electronics before he retired at eighty and my dad took over. It can be done."

"It takes money. That's what I'm trying to dig up now."

"I don't know anything about prices for commercial property in your neck of the woods. How much room and what facilities would you need?"

The two men leaned over papers on the table, scrawling designs and figures, completely immersed in their calculations. They failed to notice the annoyance on the face of Dawn Packard, whose concerns had been totally forgotten. An outside observer would have noticed that her reaction was almost identical to that of Clarice Packard when her son and Charles had been discussing plans for the Packard business. She wanted to interrupt, but couldn't think of anything to say, so she got up and flounced out of the room, heading up the stairs to her bedroom. Charles glanced up briefly at her retreating back before going back to his intense scrutiny of Keith Wall's plans.

"You'll need financing."

"Don't I know it!"

Charles had been sizing up the other man as he talked. He thought that Brian had come by his savvy in business affairs by watching his dad at work. They had been together for thirteen years before the parents divorced. Brian had absorbed a lot.

"I think I can help you in one way. I have a very good relationship with my bank. I can go to them and ask them to contact a branch in your city and listen to your plans. You

44

need a detailed business plan. I'll need a copy. Don't worry. No one will see it but myself and my banker."

"I already have one, though it will need to be finished once I have a property in mind."

"Good. Send it to me."

Keith stared in disbelief at Packard. All he could manage to say was, "Thank you. I had no idea you would be interested."

CHAPTER TEN

As Dawn Packard entered the lawyer's office, he rose and held out his hand.

"Miss Packard. Congratulations on your eighteenth birthday. I imagine you must be here to get the details on your entitlement to the legacy from your late mother."

"No, Mr. McNeill. That's not what I'm here for, though I suppose it's something I have to do. What I want to talk to you about is my brother's death. At the time of his death, I said that when I turned eighteen and became an adult I'd sue every one of the people who conspired to kill him; the doctors at the hospital and my stepmother."

Taken aback by this statement, the lawyer, who was the senior partner of a large and highly respected law firm, sank into the chair behind his desk and regarded the young woman with some trepidation. This was not the kind of case he was used to handling and it came as a complete surprise.

"I normally don't handle cases of that sort. I have been the attorney for your father for many years. It has mostly amounted to contracts for the company, the distribution of your late mother's estate, and his will. I must say, I find this somewhat distasteful. Are you sure you want to do this?"

"I am very sure. Ever since that day, I've been looking forward to the time I was old enough to act on my own. My father knows about it, but he can't stop me even if he wants to. I'm now an adult and can make my own decisions."

The lawyer noted the aggressive expression on Dawn's face and heard the firm resolve in her voice. He sighed and reached for a file that listed all the firm's partners.

"This is a large firm and we have people who are experts in a number of kinds of law. Drew Robinson has handled several medical malpractice cases and done very well. However, he is usually defending the doctors. Still, he has the experience as to how these cases unfold. I would like to refer you to him if that would be all right with you."

"That would be fine. I expected as much. Thank you."

The lawyer buzzed his secretary. "Please put me through to Mr. Robinson."

Drew Robinson, a tall, lanky black man with a small, neatly trimmed beard and a receding hairline, was often mistaken for a basketball player. Occasionally, when a young fan stopped him on the street and asked for his autograph, he would comply with an unreadable squiggle that could be interpreted as any player the youngster idolized. There was no mistaking him when he walked into a courtroom, however. He was a fearsome opponent and had built up an enviable reputation.

"I remember the incident in which your stepbrother died. I know many members of the medical profession, and when the law was being debated, I asked several of them what they thought."

"What did they say?"

"Their reaction was mixed. Some doctors, who had elderly patients who were saying they wanted to go that way, approved of the law. One told me, after the law had been passed, that when some of these patients actually confronted the possibility of euthanasia, they backed out. They hadn't the nerve to actually make the request. As far as I know, no one has actually requested euthanasia, here in this area at least. One doctor told me that the children of one old lady have been urging her to agree to it, telling her she would be with Jesus and not have any more pain. But she has dug in her heels and said no to them."

"Good for her."

"Yes. But a couple of doctors I talked to said they were afraid that heirs of senile oldsters, or parents of severely disabled children might take that route to get rid of someone who is a nuisance. It has happened in other countries where euthanasia is legal."

Robinson thought for a minute, then continued, "I had the sneaky impression that doctors who wouldn't have to do the actual act were more open to the ideas than were doctors who would actually have to do it; ones like anesthesiologists. The anesthesiology professor at the medical school is dead set against it."

"I don't think doctors who are opposed to it should have to do it."

"They don't. There's a clause in the law allowing doctors to refuse on moral grounds. But they have to refer their patients to other doctors who would."

"That's not fair."

"One doctor who is a pillar in his church, and who is opposed to euthanasia said he couldn't in good conscience make such a referral. He asked me what he could do if he was ever asked. He might not be asked, because he has signs in his waiting room to the effect that he won't agree to euthanasia, but he wanted to be prepared just in case. He cannot legally refuse to refer such a patient. I told him he could tell the patient that there are phone listings and websites that will put them in touch with a physician who will. It has never been tried in court, but I doubt if any judge would disagree with that approach."

"Did you ever talk to these doctors about what happened to Brian?"

"Yes, I did. Some felt that the benefits outweighed the cost."

"What cost? If you mean the cost of Brian's life, he was a human being with a right to live."

"I agree. But there was another cost that some doctors stressed. That was the cost of keeping him alive for a long period of time, when the space and the facilities could be used for other patients. Now, don't take this to heart," he said noting the scowl that showed on the young woman's face. "I'm only reporting what I heard. I'm not making judgments."

Dawn nodded.

"Other doctors were upset that the issue of euthanasia in order to harvest his organs was made too rapidly, and especially as it was made on a weekend when his neurosurgeon and a couple of members of the newly struck committee to study the problem presented by the new law were out of town at a major medical convention. Though some thought the question of timing was just coincidental, not planned."

"What side did you take in this argument?"

"Neither. But it gave me pause to think about the problems euthanasia might cause."

"Well, I can tell you there are lots of problems. We know all about problems."

"What, for instance?"

"Insurance companies won't pay. My stepmother and Keith—he's Brian's real dad—can't collect on his insurance. And the cops couldn't charge the guy who ran him off the road with killing him because he didn't actually die from his injuries."

"That makes sense," Robinson mused.

"It doesn't either make sense!"

"Sorry. I mean it makes sense to the insurance companies. I know it left you folks out on a limb."

"Yeah. You can say that again. Clarice never stops talking about it."

Robinson leaned back in his chair and thought for a minute. "Dawn, I notice that you refer to Clarice Packard as your stepmother, but to Brian as your brother."

"Clarice never acted like a mother to me. She never did like me. But Brian was the best big brother I could have had. In fact, I don't think Clarice liked Brian either. I think she was in a snit because Brian was so good to me."

"Still, are you sure you want to list her in this lawsuit?"

"She's the one who said yes to having him killed and signed all the forms. I hate her for that. Those doctors talked her into it, but she didn't take much persuading."

"Think of the repercussions within your family."

"I don't care. She can just pack up and go away for all I care. Dad shouldn't have ever married her."

"Then you would never have met Brian."

"And Brian wouldn't have gotten a motorcycle and would still be alive."

Robinson was getting more respect for the girl as he talked to her. She had obviously thought this out and was going to carry it through. And she would make a good witness in court.

"So will you take my case? And if you do, will you be firmly on my side?"

"Yes to both questions. I can see both sides of this question, but I don't think the law is very well written, and this case may make people think about the shortcomings of the law and do something about it. I will take on your case and do my very best. If I don't approve of what a client wants to do, I just won't take their case. But if I decide to accept the challenge, I'll put my heart and soul into it."

Dawn let out a sigh of relief. "So now what?"

"I understand that you have started a campaign to get signed petitions asking the government to repeal the law allowing euthanasia."

"I have. I have a copy with me."

Robinson accepted the sheet of paper Dawn handed over and read through it. "Okay then, you can keep up with this. Do you have help getting these petitions out?"

"A lot of my friends have helped with a booth we have at the Hillside Mall." What Dawn didn't say was that most of those friends had had enough and were now finding other things they had to do when Dawn came asking. She had been about to give up a couple of times, but when she said this to Keith Wall, in an e-mail or over the phone, he kept urging her to continue. She had begun to think he was using her without putting anything into the campaign himself. He kept telling her that he didn't have any money, but she knew that her father was helping him out with plans for expanding his business. She had no idea of the difference in running a start-up business on a shoestring and doing so when one had money in the bank and in investments.

As if these thoughts had transmitted themselves to Robinson, he asked, "My services are not cheap. If we win, we may be able to recover the costs from the defendants. But I will need money up front. I understand from McNeill that you haven't told your father that you were going to do this."

"That's right, but I have money of my own which is now mine to use. My mother was wealthy in her own right and she split her estate between Dad and myself. I can pay you."

"All right, let's get down to business. First, have you considered filing a complaint with the board that grants medical licenses?"

"Do you think that will do any good?"

"The good it will do is to get further publicity for your cause. A complaint to the medical board, even if they don't do anything, in fact, especially if they don't do anything, can help that campaign to repeal the law get off and running."

"All right, do it."

"We should include the hospital. I am not questioning the care your brother got up until that time, but the hospital is responsible for its employees."

Dawn nodded.

"The next thing I need you to do is to tell me absolutely everything you can remember about what happened. Every little detail, with times and places. You have to go over everything in your mind, look up any documents, try to remember names of everyone who was there. Don't leave anything out. Don't try to hide anything. This will take several sessions with me as your memory unfolds. Can you do that?"

"Sure."

"Good, let's get an outline done now. We can add the details later."

Not surprisingly, Clarice Packard was infuriated to the point of apoplexy. "How can your daughter do that to me? Charles, if you take her side, I'm leaving you. And when I divorce you, I'll take you for everything you've got. That girl is positively insufferable."

"Don't blame my Dad," Dawn demanded. "I've turned eighteen. I am now an adult and can do things on my own without having to kowtow to anyone else. I did this on my own. I didn't tell Dad."

"Well, if you're so grown up, you can jolly well leave home and find a place to live on your own. I don't want you around this house."

"Now hold on a minute, Clarice," Charles responded. "Dawn is still in high school. She can remain at home until she graduates."

"Well, make up your mind. Either she goes or I do."

In the end, it was decided that Dawn would go to live with her aunt, Dr. Madge Packard, a retired professor of medieval literature at the University. Both Dawn and Charles greeted this offer from Madge with relief.

Before the case came to trial, Robinson called his client. "Dawn, the hospital and its doctors have made an offer to settle out of court. It is a substantial offer financially. Are you willing to do that?"

"No. I don't want to settle. This isn't about money. I don't need money and if I get any, I'll give it to the hospice. That's where Brian should have been."

"They will probably increase their offer."

"I hope you aren't giving up."

"No way! But I have to report these things to you."

"Look, I know everyone says it isn't about money when it really is. But I have money from my mother's bequest. She was wealthy in her own right. And my Dad isn't exactly poor. So it really isn't about money. What I want is to make this whole thing as public as possible, to show the damage this euthanasia law has done, and to get it repealed. I want to avenge my brother."

"Okay. I thought that was how you would react. As for me, I'm as anxious to get this case into court as you are. I think it is extremely important. And I'm looking forward to a real donnybrook. There's going to be all the publicity you could possibly want, some of it directed at you. It will be nerve-wracking for you. Be aware of that."

"I can stand it. Just watch me!"

CHAPTER ELEVEN

The school year was approaching its end and most students in Dawn's class at Edmund Baker High were busy making plans for the upcoming year at universities and colleges. Edmund Baker was located in the area of monster homes of the very rich, of doctors, lawyers, and CEOs of major corporations. Its graduates routinely thought of post-secondary education, many with thoughts of professional schools or advanced degrees. Many went to Centralia U., but there were others fanning out over the country and foreign countries as well.

Two students were not thinking of college classes next year. Jon Smits sat on the grassy lawn of Dr. Madge Packard's house while Dawn Packard stretched out on the grass beside him.

"I've decided to take a gap year," Jon remarked. "I'd like to backpack around Europe, staying at hostels and going to some of the cultural events over there. It might be the only time for years and years that I'll get a chance to do that."

"That sounds like fun," Dawn replied in an expressionless voice.

Jon laughed. "You don't sound like that really excites you."

"Should it?"

"I just thought you might like to go too." He looked down at her hopefully.

She glanced up at him. "I can't. You know that. I have this lawsuit coming up."

Jon made a face. "I don't see why you're so keen on that. Besides, it won't come up for ages."

"But there's lots to do in advance. And I have to keep up with the petition drive. There'll be another election before long…"

"Not for a couple more years."

"Still, I want to get as many petitions signed to send in well in advance, so it will be an election subject."

"Do you really think your little petitions are going to be noticed? There's a lot of other things people are interested in when it comes to elections."

"I'll make them take notice. Just wait and see. Besides, the lawsuit will get people's interest up."

"I wish you'd give up on that stuff. I hardly see you anymore. We used to do a lot more stuff together."

"We still see each other nearly every day."

"Yeah, to say hello."

There was a long silence as each of them considered their position. Jon broke the silence. "I hope you're not upset because I wanted to have sex with you. I thought you enjoyed it when we did it."

"I liked it. What made you think I didn't?"

"I dunno. You just seem different lately."

"I'll do it with you again if you want."

"Really?"

"Yeah."

Jon leaned over and kissed her. "Let's go out to the park tonight then."

"Okay." Dawn giggled. "Bring the you-know-whats. It's the wrong time of the month to do it without."

As the time got closer to the end of the school year, Jon continued his pleas to Dawn trying to persuade her to come with him on his trip. She continued to tell him that she could not do so.

"You know, Dawn, you're changing. You're getting hard. All you think about is getting even with those people. Why don't you give it a rest? A change of scenery will do you good, get you more relaxed."

"I don't want to relax. You haven't lost a brother. You don't know what it's like. I want to stay angry until I get even. Why don't you wait another year or two, until the court case is over? Then I could go with you."

"That's no good. Once I get onto a career track, I won't be able to take time off and go gallivanting around the world. I have to do it now."

"Well, you'll have to go by yourself."

Jon let the subject drop, but when they parted, he gave her a perfunctory kiss on the cheek and walked away.

CHAPTER TWELVE

It wasn't long before another young man walked into Dawn's life. Dawn and Madge were relaxing on the back deck when the doorbell rang. Dawn hurried through the house to answer the door and found a tall, athletic-looking man in his mid-twenties standing on the front step. Handsome too, Dawn thought. She vaguely recognized him but couldn't come up with a name.

"I'm Alex Hamilton," he said in a pleasant baritone voice.

"Oh, hi. Come on in. I remember you from the Symphony gala last year."

"Right. Our dads are both directors of the Friends of the Symphony. My dad is Maxwell Hamilton."

Madge, on hearing the exchange, came to the door and invited the young man to join them on the back deck where they were having cool glasses of iced tea. "How are your mother and father these days? I haven't seen them since the gala."

"They're fine, thank you," he replied accepting the glass offered him. "I came over because I think I can help Dawn with her petition campaign."

"Really?" Madge queried, raising her eyebrows. "I thought she had already worn out most of her friends and acquaintances getting them to man her booth for her."

"I wasn't thinking of that sort of thing." He turned his attention back to Dawn. "I can help you expand and reach far more people. I'll be in my final year for my MBA next year. I can put together an action plan, and through my father, I have lots of connections. He's the CEO of Western Standard Investments, one of the largest investment companies in the country. I think we can make this expand into more areas. And we can do publicity all over the country."

"I'm sure that most of your contacts will be in favor of euthanasia, not opposed to it. It seems to be gaining in popularity," Madge remarked.

"Many people will be, but we can get publicity even through them. The more people talk about it, the better."

"I've already put it on my Facebook page and on Twitter," Dawn remarked.

"I know, but we can do a much more widely read Facebook page. You have to spend a bit of money for what I have planned, but it won't be that much."

"Just what is your motive for doing this?" Madge challenged. "Is it merely to have a project for one of your courses?"

Hamilton turned toward the professor and spoke earnestly. "No, Dr. Packard. I have a personal reason. My grandmother, Mom's mother, lives with us. She is eighty and is very frail. She can walk when she needs to, but mostly she uses a wheelchair. She is deathly afraid of being put in a nursing home for fear it will be the first step toward being considered an old person who no longer has any value to society and might be 'put down like an old dog' as she puts it. We are constantly assuring her that we would never agree to that and also that as long as she wants to stay at home, she is welcome at our house. She has a nurse in the daytime, and at night we care for her. Mom is very adamant that she will always care for her, no matter what she needs. But she still worries. She thinks that even if she has to go to the hospital, they might not treat her like they would a younger person, and might just let her die."

"I see."

"When can we get started on this new plan?" Dawn broke in, her voice full of enthusiasm. "Every once in a while I think I'll give up, but when I say that to Brian's dad, he sort of berates me for quitting."

"I don't know him. Does he live here?"

"Oh no. He's way back east. But we talk back and forth on the phone or Twitter all the time."

"By the way, I haven't had the chance to personally tell you how sad I was to learn of Brian's death in such tragic circumstances. I was at his funeral, but didn't get a chance to speak to you."

"Did you know him?"

"Yes. We were in school together, at Baker. We were in the same graduating class, but we were interested in different subjects. But I knew him and I remember him as a nice kid. I think it was tragic what happened to him."

"You're right about that. I'm suing those people who agreed to having him killed."

Hamilton winced a bit at Dawn's choice of words. "I heard about that."

For the next half hour the two young people were busy discussing and planning. Madge left them to it, having assured herself that Alex Hamilton was on the up-and-up and had no evil designs on her young niece.

CHAPTER THIRTEEN

At the end of the school year, Dawn Packard went to work full-time for her father. For the previous two years she had worked as a gofer in the department that filled orders for merchandise. The big orders to large TV or computer companies were filled elsewhere, but every day, orders were sent out to small manufacturers or to stores and repair shops for the electronic components of a variety of devices. This year the woman in charge was off on maternity leave, and Charles felt that his daughter had enough know-how to fill in for the summer. She took orders, then sent the two youths who pulled the supplies off the shelves out to fill the orders. She checked that the orders were correct and sent them off to shipping to be packaged and shipped.

One of the gofers was turning out to be a nuisance. Kyle Quigley had been in Dawn's class at Baker High, but Dawn did not know him. Dawn had been in the advanced group where the top students were preparing for academic careers. Kyle had not. Dawn showed the two recruits where to find things, how to read the product codes, and emphasized that they must not only check the labels on the shelves, but also on the product when they removed it from the shelf. Kyle took much longer than the other youth in learning the system, and Dawn frequently had to go with him to get the correct product. After several days of this, he started coming to her to ask where to get a certain item, explaining that he did not want to make a mistake. She was taking far too much time working with him, but with patience she continued to try to train him. She complained to her father one evening when they had gone out to dinner.

"You can't expect all of them to learn things as quickly as you did," her father counseled. "Be patient with him."

At the end of one working morning, she tried a new tactic, that of sitting him down at her cubbyhole and explaining again as clearly as she could the product codes and how they were arranged on the shelves. At the end of her lecture, he remarked, "Thanks a lot. Hey, how about going out for a burger."

"Okay," she replied.

There was a lunch counter across the street from the Packard plant. They had burgers and fries and made small talk until it was time to go back to work. Dawn opened her purse to pay for her burger, but Kyle said hastily, "No, no. I'm paying for this." Dawn realized that Kyle thought of their meeting as a date and was none too pleased. But she decided to politely thank him and never go out to lunch with him again.

Kyle continued to find ways to talk to Dawn or have to ask her questions. Finally, she had had enough and told him so. From then on, when he came to her for any reason, she gave him the cold shoulder.

Dawn dated several young men, including Dave Brewster, a classmate at Baker High. She liked the big, friendly football player and spent considerable time with him. She had more free time now that Alex Hamilton had taken over the petition program. Alex seemed to regard their relationship as a purely business one, to Dawn's disappointment. They met frequently, but never dated. Madge Packard realized that Alex was too much older than Dawn and probably had other women nearer his age to squire around, but Charles only heard his daughter enthuse about Alex and approved. He was in the correct social class, to Charles' way of thinking.

Alex had set up a little office in the Hillside Mall. One of the volunteers made a big, gaudy sign. It was a somewhat outrageous piece of art that had little to do with euthanasia, but was an eye-catcher that brought people's attention to the remainder of the message. Inside, a large poster showing Brian Wall as a healthy, happy young man was prominently displayed on the back wall, where it was seen by everyone who walked in the door. Customers at the mall flocked in to see what it was all about. Only a few signed the petition, but everyone seemed to want to stay and talk. Every day, you could count on lively discussions, and everyone went away with information, much of which was new to them. As Alex pointed out, that was as important as the petitions. Most favored the legalization of euthanasia, as Alex had expected, but at least they had been shown that there was another side to the question.

The lawsuit was a ways off yet and there was nothing to do at the moment in regard to it.

Jon Smits sent weekly updates about his travels through Europe, with selfies taken in front of well-known tourist attractions. She was only one of half a dozen former classmates he included in his e-mails, which annoyed her, failing to realize that she had only herself to blame.

Whenever she did not contact Keith Wall for a period of time, he would call her to see how things were coming, constantly urging her on, stoking up her anger toward the people she felt had killed her brother. She was impatient for the summer to end. The court date had been set for September. She wanted to get it over with and was frustrated when a delay was granted.

One of the defendants, the second doctor to approve the euthanasia of Brian Wall, the one referred to by the others as "Dr. Death," suffered a massive heart attack and died. Dawn had not known about this man, though her father and stepmother did. His name had been unfamiliar to her until her lawyer had dug up the information that it had not been Martin Schumacher who had, along with Steve Mendel, signed the approval papers for Brian's euthanasia. Schumacher had been retained on the list of defendants, since it had been his opinion that there was no chance for the youth to recover from his injuries that the other two doctors had used for their approval, and perhaps just as importantly, to persuade the family to agree.

The defense team asked for time to rearrange their plans as a result of the death of one of the defendants. The new date was set for November.

CHAPTER FOURTEEN

The courtroom was filled to capacity, and prominent among the spectators were several severely disabled people in wheelchairs. Room had been made for a few of them, but the ones who could not get in placed themselves quietly on either side of the courtroom door, a constant reminder that disabled people were adamantly opposed to the euthanasia bill, fearing that it might be used against them when they could no longer handle their own affairs.

Clarice Packard, dressed stylishly and expensively, but ruining the impression she made by wearing an ugly scowl, glared at the wheelchairs and complained loudly to her lawyer, "Tell them to get those people out of here. They have no business being here. This is nothing to do with them."

"They have the right of every citizen to come to court to observe a trial." To himself, the lawyer observed, *it's called freedom.* He cautioned her, "If I were you, I'd keep those thoughts to yourself. You don't want to give them a cause for complaint."

Clarice had moved out of the Packard house and was living in an expensive apartment, paid for by Charles, who was torn between the demands of his wife and those of his daughter. He sat quietly among the spectators, not wanting to call attention to himself, but giving Dawn an encouraging smile when she looked his way.

The two doctors were a contrast. Martin Schumacher wore a navy blue suit, light blue shirt and tie. Steve Mendel rushed in at the last moment, straight from the hospital, wearing a coat over blue surgical scrubs. Tomorrow, when he had to testify, he would come in suit and tie, but today, he would only sit in the back and listen. The hospital administrator was very proper and conservative. With a brief nod to his lawyer, he also took a back seat.

The jurors having been selected, the testimony began with an account of the accident that had injured Brian Wall. The contractor who had been following Wall and had stayed on the scene to give first aid turned out to be an excellent witness, recounting the events that led up to the crash with precision and accuracy, and describing the spinning motorcycle crashing into the youth's head. It was obvious from his testimony that the accident had not been Brian's fault, but had been caused by the recklessness of the sports car driver, though it seemed apparent that the car had not actually collided with the bike. That would be meat for a defense lawyer if this had been a criminal trial for the driver of the car, but was not of concern in this trial.

One of the defense attorneys leaned over and whispered to another. "I wonder why the Packard girl isn't going after that other driver?"

Testimony was heard from the paramedics and the ER staff. There was no doubt that Brian Wall had received exemplary care from everyone involved on that day. Some of the jurors seemed a bit squeamish when the injuries were described and photos of them shown. When the images of the CT scans were shown, there were blank stares from the jurors. Many had seen X-rays, or photos of them, but the strange images on the CT scan, showing the fractured skull and the bleeding into the brain, were unintelligible to them. Dr. Bentley, who had taken over the young man's treatment after the ER staff had stabilized him, was next to be called to the stand. He was established as an expert witness in his specialty of neurosurgery.

"Dr. Bentley, is it possible that Brian Wall could have recovered from his injuries?"

"Yes, it would have been possible, though his injuries were very serious and he might well have died."

"If he had regained consciousness, could he have lived a normal life?'

"He might have had serious challenges to overcome, but it is a possibility, yes."

"Would the fact that he was young, healthy and physically fit as a former athlete be in his favor?"

"Most definitely yes."

"Thank you."

One of the defense attorneys bore down on the doctor.

"Isn't it true, that he was very likely to die?"

"Yes, though that was not inevitable."

"But you told the family to expect the worst and be prepared for his death."

"Of course. They needed to know that death was a possibility."

"A probability, in fact."

"A probability, but not inevitable."

"Just give me a yes or no answer, doctor. It could be expected that he would die."

"Yes, but…"

"Thank you doctor. That is all."

The next witness was the Packards' family physician.

"How long had Brian Wall been a patient of yours?"

"For eight years."

"So you knew him fairly well."

"Oh, yes."

"Was he in good health?"

"Excellent health in every way."

"Was he physically fit?"

"Indeed he was."

"Was he ever injured?"

"He received injuries from playing football twice."

"How did he react to those injuries?"

"He followed instructions, did the rehab work required of him, and healed very rapidly."

"If he had recovered consciousness from this accident, do you think that he would have had the physical and mental capability of overcoming any obstacles to his recovery?"

"Head injuries are not really in my field of expertise, but as far as his mental attitude was concerned, he would have worked very hard at his rehab."

"Do you think he should have been given a longer time to see if he would regain consciousness?"

"I do."

The defense attorney bored in. "Doctor, you say that you are not a specialist in head injuries."

"That is correct."

"That is all, doctor." The lawyer sat down, a smirk on his face.

Keith Wall flew in to testify at the trial and planned to stay to the end to support Dawn, who he now treated like a daughter. He described his dismay at calling his son, only to learn that the boy was dead, and how when he arrived at the Packard home, he was also told of the decision by his ex-wife to allow euthanasia. He related his utter devastation at the news. He and Brian had kept in touch, and he had been proud of his son's achievements. He had been delighted to learn of Brian's opportunities at Packard Electronics. He was appalled at his son's life being snuffed out in such a cavalier fashion. He told of his visit to the hospital administrator, with its accusation of incompetence that the hospital had not informed him when his injured son had been admitted. At the end of his testimony, he broke down in tears. Cross-examination was put off until the next day.

Dawn was the last witness called. She described in detail the days and hours from the time the family was allowed to see the injured youth until she was dragged away by the security personnel. Robinson did not ask her about her comments made in her extreme distress. He had cautioned her that the defense would bring them up and had coached her on controlling her temper and not being lured into saying anything that she would regret later. "Stick to the truth and don't say anything other than a direct answer to the question asked," he had told her.

One of the defense lawyers, a large, imposing man, opened the questioning. "You keep calling Brian Wall your brother. He isn't, is he?"

"Brian is my brother."

73

"Your stepbrother."

"He is my brother. He is legally my brother and we lived in the same house as brother and sister."

"I understand you and he couldn't get along."

"That's not true. We got along just fine. We were very close."

"That's not what I've heard. He called you names and made nasty comments about you."

"That was just teasing. He would call me "funny face" or "piggy nose" because my nose turns up a bit. I would pretend to be angry and call him a jerk. But it was all in fun. That's how Brian and I were. We were having fun!"

"He played tricks on you."

"Yes. And I did to him. Never anything nasty, and we'd end up laughing enough to split our sides."

"What did he ever do to show that he cared about you?"

That was Dawn's cue and she took it. "Once when he had only recently moved in with us, I got sick and he would bring me food and sit around and joke with me to get me to eat it. And one time when there had been a scare about some guy trying to pick up little girls, he walked me to school and back home even though his own school was in a different direction. Then when some boys were bullying me, he told them to leave me alone, and they did. He was always doing things like that for me. It was so nice having a big brother who cared about me."

Dawn momentarily lost control and started to sob, but pulled herself together again and stated firmly, "If you think the way I acted at the hospital when Brian was there, after his accident, that I was just a schitzy little kid, think again. I loved

74

my brother and didn't want him to die. They didn't give him a chance!"

"You did well," Robinson told Dawn after her cross-examination was over and court had adjourned for the day. "The jury liked you and they like Keith Wall. But don't get all excited. It isn't over yet. Tomorrow, it's the defense's turn. They get to tell their story."

"You're wonderful!" Dawn exclaimed, pulling him down to her level and planting a kiss on his cheek. The lawyer was pleased, but slightly embarrassed, especially as some people passing by paused for a good chuckle at the tall, black lawyer and the small blonde girl. Keith Wall, who had regained his poise came over and gave Dawn a big hug.

"Come out to dinner with me. I promise not to talk about the case. I just want to do something for my new daughter."

Madge Packard answered the phone. It had been agreed between her and her niece that she should screen the calls. There had been two very obscene calls, probably from the same man. There had also been a poison-pen letter and nasty letters to the editor of the paper.

"For you." She held the phone out to Dawn.

"Hello."

"Hi there. I'm here at the petition office and Alex says you need to sign a letter. He's busy, so I said I'd take it to you and get it signed and bring it back. Can you meet me at the bus stop there near your house? I can take the bus up and get off on the other side of the street and come across and get the letter signed and take the bus back again. I'll get there about five minutes to ten."

"Okay. I'll be there. Thanks for taking the trouble to do that."

"Who was that?" Madge asked.

"One of the guys who's helping out with our petitions. Alex needs a letter signed, so this guy is bringing it up. I kind of recognize his voice, but can't quite put a face to it. Anyway, I'll be back in ten minutes."

"I'm about to go to bed. Be sure to bolt the door when you come in."

"Sure thing Aunt Madge," Dawn said as she slipped into a jacket.

The next morning, as Drew Robinson walked down the corridor toward the courtroom, he saw the defense team huddled together in earnest discussion. He ambled over.

"Hey you guys! Are you willing to throw in the towel yet?"

They turned to stare at him.

"Haven't you heard?"

"Heard what?"

"That girl who got murdered at that bus stop last night was your client, the plaintiff."

CHAPTER FIFTEEN

While it was still dark that morning, the garbage man had rolled his big truck down Hill Street and halted near the bus stop to empty a garbage container. He noticed a yellow plastic raincoat lying on top of a heap behind the bus stop bench. In case it was a stray bit of trash, he walked down to investigate. He saw legs protruding from the bottom of the raincoat and leaned down to lift the near end, expecting to find a drunk sleeping it off. What he saw made him drop the garment and run back to his truck, where he called the office. They called the police and relayed the police instructions to the truck driver to stay where he was and not touch anything. They didn't need to tell him that. He wasn't about to go back and look at that corpse. He waited where he was until the police arrived. White-faced and shaking, he motioned toward the bench, then leaned over the edge of his garbage truck and heaved up his breakfast.

The officer from the patrol car also took a look and called for help. Before long, police cars surrounded the place.

One disgorged the two detectives assigned to the case. They gingerly lifted the plastic coat. It was a young woman, probably a teenager, long blonde hair streaming in wild array around her face. They saw a diagonal slash across her face that had bled freely, and bruises on the front of her throat. She had also been stabbed in the abdomen several times, and had been kicked in the head. They could see the imprint of the toe of a shoe on the right side of her forehead, and a large, abraded area on the left side where her head had struck the concrete leg of the bench. The body was very cold, the exposed legs of her slacks soaked by the heavy rain that had fallen during the night. They dropped the plastic coat back onto the body to await the scene of crime crew and the police doctor.

The detectives, Al Rankin and Stan Kalinski, interviewed the garbage truck driver and let him go on his way. A gray drizzle, giving the early morning light a ghostly appearance, was punctuated by the banging of garbage cans as the truck continued down the street.

The police strung crime scene tape around the area and held up two people who arrived to take the bus, due in a few minutes. One officer herded them up the sidewalk a ways and stepped out into the street to flag down the bus. He told the driver that they would set up a temporary bus stop up the road a ways and to tell that to any other driver on this route. The bus driver nodded, then asked, "What happened?"

"There's been a murder. We'll have this area cordoned off all day."

The bus had picked up several nurses from St. Luke's hospital who had come off the night shift. They craned their necks as the bus rolled slowly past the bus stop, but could see nothing. The police were erecting a tent over the site to protect it from the rain.

A city crew arrived with barricades, and after asking one resident to move his car off the street, created a new bus stop.

The doctor, Dr. Wynne Laird, arrived. When he lifted the plastic coat, he grimaced. "Whoever did this was really angry. He wanted this girl dead all right."

"So, we look for someone who quarreled with her?" Stan Kalinski asked.

"Not necessarily." Dr. Laird looked up at the young detective. "It might be someone who really hated women, or perhaps he saw a girl standing out here and thought she was a prostitute and hated her for that, or got angry when he tried to pick her up and she told him what she thought of him."

"She may have been a prostitute."

"Hmm. I suppose one could hang out up here. Wouldn't it be more likely that she would be down at the mall?"

The detectives let that slide. They watched the routine examination as the doctor worked. When he straightened up and dropped the coat back over the body, he said. "She's been choked, but that didn't kill her. She's been stabbed in the abdomen several times, slashed across the face and kicked in the head. She hit her head on the concrete leg of the bench. Now don't ask me what killed her. That will have to wait for the autopsy. But she bled after she was slashed, so she was alive for a time after that. Time of death—several hours ago. We can give you a better time later, but rigor is fully developed. I'd say yesterday evening sometime but can't be more precise than that."

When the detectives could finally get access to the pockets of the jacket the girl was wearing, they found a small purse containing, among other things, a driver's license in the name of Dawn Packard, with an address on Elm Street, a few blocks away. Rankin, the older of the two detectives asked his partner, "Isn't she the Packard heiress who's suing the hospital?"

"Yeah. They're right in the middle of the trial."

"Not a prostitute then." Rankin riffled through the cards in her wallet. They included ones from two high-end stores of the type where he never shopped.

"Just what we don't need. High society corpse and all kinds of suspects who have scads of money. Not our usual kind of case. Anyway, this address is not far from here. I guess we go there with the bad news."

CHAPTER SIXTEEN

Madge Packard was still in her dressing gown when she opened the door to the two policemen. They identified themselves as Detectives Rankin and Kalinski and showed their identification. Madge let them in, a puzzled expression on her face.

"Mrs. Packard?" Rankin inquired.

"I'm Dr. Madge Packard," she replied crisply.

"Are you Dawn Packard's mother?"

"I'm her aunt. Why?"

"Does she live here?"

"Yes. Why?" she asked sharply.

"Is she at home?"

"I assume so. She hasn't gotten up yet, so I imagine she is still sleeping."

"Mrs. Packard…"

"Dr. Packard."

"Sorry. Dr. Packard, could you go look and see if she is here?"

A thought flashed through Madge's mind. When she had opened the door to the policemen, the dead bolt had not been shot into place. Maybe Dawn had not come home last night after all. "I'll check," she murmured uncertainly and hastened to the stairs. Running up them, she called out to Dawn and when she reached the girl's room she didn't bother knocking, but pushed the door open. There was no one in the room and the bed had not been slept in. Now filled with the portent of impending disaster, she returned more slowly to the living room where the detectives waited.

"She isn't home." Madge slumped into a chair, waiving the men to sit down. They however, remained standing.

"Dr. Packard, a young woman was found dead at the bus stop on Hill Street and we found Dawn's identification with this address in her pocket."

"Oh, no! I shouldn't have let her go." She buried her face in her hands and tried to get control of her feelings. She didn't want to look like an idiot in front of the policemen.

"Go where?"

"Dawn got a phone call last night and went out to meet the person at the bus stop."

"Do you know who it was?" Rankin had seated himself opposite the woman, who was wiping her eyes with a tissue.

"No. I answered the phone because Dawn had been getting obscene phone calls and I didn't want her to have to listen to the man if that was who was calling." The two men exchanged glances at this news.

"Had she reported this?"

Madge shrugged. "No. We rather expected it because there are a lot of people who oppose her efforts to get the euthanasia law repealed. There has been a poison pen letter also, as well as nasty letters to the editor of the paper."

"Let's go back to the phone call. You say that you answered it. Then what?"

"It didn't sound like the nasty caller, so I called Dawn to the phone."

"Was it a man or a woman?"

"I thought it was a woman, but after Dawn talked to him, she said 'him' when she referred to the caller. I imagine it could have been either a man with a high-pitched voice, or a woman with a deep voice."

"Did Dawn recognize the caller?"

"She said his voice sounded familiar and she thought it was someone connected with her petition campaign. She is trying to get petitions to send to people in office to get the law allowing euthanasia repealed. She's been doing that since her brother died. Actually her stepbrother. Anyway, he apparently wanted her to meet him at the bus stop because he had a letter that Alex Hamilton, who is helping her, needed to have signed. It didn't seem to be out of the ordinary for her. Neither of us saw any danger."

"Did you check the phone number the obscene calls were made from?" Rankin asked, hoping that Dr. Packard had thought to save it.

"No. I'm old-fashioned. I use my phone strictly for making and receiving phone calls. It doesn't have any of these options that young people seem to think essential on their phones. I did save the poison pen letter, however."

"Good. Keep it, and don't handle it any more than you can help. We may want to get it from you, but that can wait."

Dr. Packard nodded her assent.

"Is Charles Packard of Packard Electronics her father?"

"Yes he is. Oh, God. He's got to be told."

"Yes ma'am. Where does he live?"

"Look. He's living alone now that wife of his has left him. I'd better go to him. Can you give me five minutes to get dressed and take me there with you?"

She was true to her word and within five minutes was dressed in slacks and sweater, had combed her hair but had not bothered with makeup, and was ready to go. She gave the men the address and sat back in the car seat without saying another word until they pulled up at the Packards' large old house, set back from the street and surrounded with trees now showing only bare branches, dripping water from the night's rain. Obvious money here, Kalinski thought.

Charles Packard let them in, a look of surprise on his face as he saw the two detectives. Madge ran to him, embraced him in a hug and sobbed, "Dawn's dead. Oh, Charles, it's so horrible."

Charles' answer was for the two men, rather than his sister, who he held firmly. "What happened?"

"I'm sorry to have to tell you, but we think that your daughter was the young woman we found murdered this morning. We found her identification on her, with the address on Elm Street, so we went there to verify that she lived there."

"And I went up to her room to look for her and she wasn't home. Oh Charles, it's my fault. I shouldn't have let her go out."

Charles' face went chalk white and the hand holding onto his sister began to shake. In a weak voice, he said, "Madge, honey, you couldn't have stopped her. She's an adult now, as she keeps reminding us. Where was she going?"

"She went out to meet some guy who had a letter or something that Alex Hamilton wanted signed. She was supposed to meet him at the bus stop on Hill Street."

Packard looked at Rankin. "Is that where she was killed?"

"Yes, it was."

"Was it Alex that she was going to meet? I don't understand."

"No. It was someone else, I don't know who," Madge answered.

"Sir, we don't know that it was the man she went to meet who killed her," cautioned Rankin. "It might have been a legitimate meeting that went off okay, but someone else came along after that man had left." Kalinski appreciated the fact that Rankin had not mentioned the second alternative, that the man had come across the girl's dead body and had fled in a panic, not wanting to become involved. Rankin might seem tough when you talked to him, but he had a soft side also that occasionally showed in situations like this.

"You haven't told me how she died," Packard said.

"She was stabbed, and possibly choked," Rankin answered.

Packard collapsed onto the couch, his face showing a combination of horror and confusion. "What happens now?" he asked weakly.

"We will need you to come down to the morgue to identify her."

Packard groaned. "Can I go now? Let's get it over with."

"We'll take you down to the morgue and bring you back."

"Do you want me to come with you, Charles?"

"No. Stay here till I get back. This is something I have to do myself."

CHAPTER SEVENTEEN

Returning to the crime scene, where people clad from head to foot in white coveralls were combing the ground and picking up anything they found, Rankin, the senior of the two detectives, asked, "Any sign of the knife?"

A shake of the head. "He must have taken it away with him. He didn't leave it here and we looked along the street, on both sides, up and down. No knife."

"You know, I think we screwed up here."

"In what way?" Kalinski asked.

"I let that garbage collector go and I remember him going off down the road emptying all the garbage cans. And I seem to recall later that I heard some banging down that way and saw another truck, one of the ones that empty those big dumpsters, pull out of the parking lot by that bar down there, that Checkers Pub."

"So our precious knife has probably already been compacted into a bale and hauled off to wherever the city dumps it."

"Yeah."

One of the white-clad crime scene officers came over. "I can tell you one other thing." He gestured toward a group of shrubs under an overhanging tree limb. "Your guy stood over there to wait."

The detectives viewed the area, noting some impressions in the earth.

"Not enough there now to get impressions from footprints, but he stood there. That rain last night was pretty heavy and it washed away a lot of stuff. It washed almost all the blood off that raincoat. There must have been blood there from that wound on the face, even if the other cuts didn't bleed much externally. He dropped the coat over the body with the outside up, so the rain gave it a thorough wash."

"Anything on the inside of the coat?"

"Don't know yet. We packed it up and sent it to the lab. We saved some blood-tinged rainwater also. By the way, this happened before it started to rain. When they removed the body, the ground was dry underneath."

Rankin thanked the officer and turned to Kalinski. "Set up a house-to-house, and have someone go to that pub and see if the staff there can remember any of the customers who were there last night. Have them make a list of any they know by name."

"You know," Kalinski mused, "the guy who did this doesn't need to be the same as the one who called to ask her to meet him here, like you told Packard."

"Hmm. I guess not."

"I've been wondering about the person who stood over there behind the bushes. The guy who called wouldn't have had to wait."

"Yeah, but she might have got there late."

"I gathered from what the aunt said, she went right out. The guy who called could have come, got the letter signed and caught the bus back, or decided to walk on down to the mall. Or he could have come after it happened, saw her body and decided to scram."

"Could be. We'll just have to wait till we talk to the bus driver. In the meantime, we need to get onto the weather office to see when it started raining."

CHAPTER EIGHTEEN

If you looked at the two detectives you might well think that Kalinski, the large, slow-moving man with somewhat baggy clothes was the one who had worked his way up from a cop on the beat and that Rankin, the smaller, more dapper man, was the one with a degree in police science. But you would be wrong. Kalinski, when he was not on duty, was the one with his nose in a book. How this mismatched pair could work so well together puzzled their fellow officers. The bond between them came from each man recognizing the value that the other brought to the combination and the willingness to combine their efforts for a more productive whole.

Al Rankin's father had been a policeman also. He had retired only a few years ago, full of honors, with a splendid sendoff from his fellow officers. They thought enough of him to want to give him something more than just a watch. So they gave him a grandfather clock! The huge clock now had pride of place in the living room of Gus Rankin's split level in a new subdivision on the west side of town.

The son had a more modest twenty-year-old house in an older area, but one that had escaped the deterioration of the more central areas of the city. Al Rankin had been lucky in finding a young woman who was not daunted by the erratic hours of a detective's life. She took all the cancelled vacations and screwed up plans in stride and gave him two children; a son who was now studying to be a lawyer and a daughter starting training to be a nurse. He had always known he would become a cop, like his father. He started out pounding a beat in the rundown center of town, peering down dark alleys, checking the back doors of businesses to be sure they were locked, hauling drunks off to the clink to dry out and breaking up bar fights.

He had showed a quick mind and an ability to remember and collate random pieces of information that caused his superiors to suggest he apply for the detective division.

Stan Kalinski's parents had immigrated after the Second World War. All their six children had been born here in Centralia. Stan was the third son, the fifth child of a city worker, one of the thankless men who plowed the snow in winter, mended broken water lines and flushed the sewers.

There had been only one special moment in Mike Kalinski's years at work. He had been on call one bitterly cold Christmas Day, and had been called out at seven in the morning to fix a broken water main. Because of the severe cold, the ground was frozen hard. It was slow, tiring work just to get down to the source of the problem. The water had to be turned off to the whole neighborhood, which ruined the plans of housewives all down the street. Some women, however scrounged around and found ways to give their families their morning coffee and to bring steaming cups of coffee and hot chocolate to the weary workers who were working without any breaks to get the pipe repaired. It was noon before the water could be turned back on. As it flowed through the new pipe, while the workers held their breath, no new leaks were detected, and the men set to filling up the hole.

Several days later, a card came in the mail thanking him for the work they had done to rescue what remained of Christmas. It was signed by several families in the area where the crew had been working. Mr. Kalinski, deeply moved by this, the only recognition he ever had of the essential work he did, had the card framed and hung it on the wall.

Stan's parents noticed that he was different from the older children. At six years of age, he was reading at fourth grade level, and at five he had put together an adult-level jigsaw puzzle in half the time it had taken his mother. The whole family had at that time lived in a small house that could have been put in the living room of some of the big houses up on the hillside. He attended school in the tough neighborhood near the old center of town, where teachers noticed his talents and gave him extra attention. He was a pleasant child, never getting into trouble, and the teachers viewed him as they would a rose in a dandelion patch. Once in high school, he was pushed to go on to college, but the family finances might not have allowed this extravagance.

However, the older siblings were also proud of the accomplishments of their younger brother, and the family got together to scrape up enough money to help make him the first family member ever to go to college. A couple of small scholarships, and a student loan and he was off to further his studies. He had been fascinated by articles and books about true crime and wanted to become a policeman, but one with a degree in police science. Centralia U. did not offer that course of study, so he had to go farther afield. He returned in four years with his degree, with honors, and was accepted into the police force.

He started by cruising the streets in a patrol car in order to get experience, but was soon transferred to the detective division. By some quirk of scheduling, he was assigned to work with Rankin, very much the opposite in education and experience. To everyone's amazement, they found they could work well together, and Rankin asked to have the young recruit assigned to work with him on a regular basis.

Rankin leaned back in his office chair to review their findings so far. Clad in coordinated browns (his wife's doing), his sandy hair neatly combed and slicked down, he looked more like a banker than a policeman. Kalinski had shucked his jacket and perched himself on the corner of his desk. His shirt threatened to escape its confines, and he had loosened his tie and undone the top button of his shirt. His bushy black hair defied all his efforts to keep it neat.

"Packard identified her all right. They cleaned her up pretty well, but it was still an ugly sight with that big gash across her face," Rankin observed. "Someone sure didn't like that little girl. No sign of sexual interference though."

"One thing for her dad to be thankful about."

"Okay, who do we have for suspects?"

Kalinski enumerated them on his fingers. "First the family."

Rankin grimaced. "I know we have to investigate them, but I can't really see the father or the aunt in that role."

"The aunt had the best opportunity."

"Yeah, she did. She could have made up that whole rigmarole about the phone call. But I can't see any motive for the father or the aunt.

"The stepmother hated the girl's guts."

"Right. She blames the girl for breaking up the marriage, according to the newspaper."

"Yeah. And she's in the next category. Lawsuit defendants. Those two doctors and the hospital administrator."

"I think you can leave the administrator out. Hospitals have lawsuits filed against them all the time. Whenever someone doesn't get totally well in minutes, they blame the doctor or the hospital. It's all in a day's work for that guy."

"Those two doctors are different. Schumacher wasn't one of the doctors who signed the papers to have the kid euthanized. Some other doctor did, but he's dead now. But Schumacher apparently is the one who told the others that the kid was going to die anyway. I think the two who signed the papers relied on his diagnosis. According to the reports, he's the one the Packard girl zeroed in on. He was the bad guy in her opinion."

"I wonder if he was not mentally stable. Would that be enough to kill the girl in such a brutal way?"

Kalinski merely shrugged. Going on with his list of suspects, he said, "Okay, next—boyfriends."

"We'll have to ask the father and the aunt about that. Anyone else?"

"The obscene caller, the poison pen letter writer and the people who write letters to the editor."

"At least with the latter group we have names. The others will be hard to trace. Fortunately the aunt had the common sense to keep the letter."

"So where do we start?"

"We talk to those two doctors, Schumacher and Mendel." Rankin made a face. "I'll take the stepmother. I'll also see the brother's dad, Keith Wall."

"I forgot about him. Can't see a motive."

"Well, you never know, so I'll mosey over and talk to him. Probably best to wait till evening to interview the doctors. In the meantime, we heard from the bus company. The driver who was on that bus route last night comes on duty at two-thirty. You go down there and talk to him. He starts out at the main downtown stop. After you finish there, go over to the morgue. The pathologist is going to do the autopsy this afternoon. I'll talk to Mrs. Packard and then see if I can find Keith Wall."

CHAPTER NINETEEN

"Yes, I was on the Hill Street route last night. How can I help you?"

"As you probably know, a body was found this morning at the last stop above the mall," Kalinski explained. "She had been dead for several hours and was probably killed late last night."

"It must have been after I came down on my last run, if she was killed there. I didn't see anything."

"It happened there all right. Can you describe your route for me?"

"Sure. I leave here at half past the hour. It's a fifty-five minute run altogether. I go up to the Hillside Mall then up Hill Street. Near the top, I go around some of the side streets and end up at St. Luke's on the hour. It's a timed stop. I can't leave there until on the hour, straight up. I come down Hill and have another timed stop at the mall. I leave there at twelve minutes after the hour, and get back down here at twenty-five after."

"Were you right on schedule last night?"

"Possibly a bit ahead of schedule. There aren't so many people who ride the bus that late. I had several that I let off on the way up, and picked up one person at the hospital, but I didn't pick up any more till I got to the mall. Then I picked up a bunch at the mall. There was a hockey game at the arena last night and it had just got out. I was a little ahead of time getting to the mall, but like I said, I had to wait till twelve after to leave there."

"That's the last run of the night, I take it."

"Yes."

"Now, let's concentrate on the last bus stop above the mall, about a block or two up from the Checkers Pub."

The driver nodded.

"Did you stop at the bus stop across the street on your way up?"

"Yeah, I let two people off there."

"Can you describe them?"

"Hey, I'm not much good at that. Anyway, they were both regular riders. I don't know their names, but they live near there. One went on up the street and the other up a side street."

Men or women?"

"One of each."

"Did the man cross the street?"

"No, he went on up the same side."

"On your way back, did you see anyone there, either at the stop, or near it?"

A shake of the head. "There wasn't anyone waiting for the bus. That's all I looked for. I didn't look to see if there was anyone else near there."

"Did you see anyone walking along the sidewalk?"

"Like I said, I didn't look."

"And did you see anything on the ground at the bus stop."

"Same answer. I didn't look."

"Thanks. That's clear enough. One more question. Was it raining when you came by there?"

The driver thought a minute. "Not then. I remember that it was starting to sprinkle when I left the mall. I had to turn on my wipers. Then a couple of minutes later it started to pour."

"About a quarter after ten, then?"

"Yeah, that's about right."

"Okay. Thanks for your help."

The driver nodded and climbed onto his bus.

CHAPTER TWENTY

Stan Kalinski had only observed a few autopsies and they still turned his stomach. The pathologist offered him a disposable mask and he accepted gratefully. The place was clean, almost to the point of being aseptic, but it still stank. He thought of it as the smell of death.

X-rays showed a fractured hyoid bone in the neck, a common injury with strangulation. So considerable force had been applied, but the pathologist told Kalinski that death had not been caused by strangulation. Some of the other signs of that sort of death were lacking. When the body was rolled over, a horizontal bruise on the back of the neck was evident.

"Did it look as if she had fallen onto something, like the back of the bench?" the pathologist asked.

"No, the bench didn't have a back, just the seat."

The pathologist examined the bruise intently, then murmured, "Karate chop, I'd say. Used to stun her so she wouldn't cry out while he grabbed for her neck."

"If he came up behind her, she might not have had a chance to cry out."

"He didn't though. Look at these bruises on the front of the neck. She was choked from in front. Also, no defensive injuries. No knife wounds on the hands or skin under the nails. Caught by surprise and disabled by the blow to the neck."

"Can you tell whether that was before or after the slash across the face?"

"Oh, before unquestionably. There is no smearing of the blood. It would have been smeared all around the neck and in the hair if she'd been bleeding at the time she was choked. She was kicked after she started bleeding however. Some of the blood was driven into the wound by the toe of the boot. I can tell you one thing; she was kicked by a leather-soled shoe or boot. See the mark here."

"Not a Nike or Reebok then."

"No. Here's the place her head hit the leg of the bench. The radiographs showed a slight skull fracture in this area. A lot of force! He really hauled off and let go with his kick. We'll find brain damage on both sides of the head."

"Just like her brother. His injuries were on both sides of the brain according to the report we got."

"Not the same. Different mechanism."

"How so?"

"I did the autopsy on that young man also, you know. He received a very hard blow on the right side. It cracked his brand new, high quality motorcycle helmet. The damage to the left side of his brain was not caused by a direct blow, as we have here. The brain is a very soft organ and is suspended and cushioned on all sides by the cerebrospinal fluid. When there is a blow on one side of the head, the brain bounces across and impacts the inside of the skull on the other side. Two injuries with a single blow."

The pathologist straightened up and looked directly at the young detective. "It wasn't in my report, but I can tell you this. That young man would not have lived. In the rare chance he might have regained some sort of consciousness, he would have been far from normal."

"A sort of zombie?"

"I guess you could say so. He would have died within a few days, so it did him no injustice to take his life and harvest his organs."

"It sure caused a lot of problems for his family though."

"I'm sure it did."

"If he had been allowed to die on his own, could his organs still be transplanted?"

"Oh, yes."

"Do you think they should have waited until he died naturally?"

"Off the record, yes I do. Does that mean that I'm opposed to euthanasia? No. I think there is a place for it, but this one case showed up everything that could go wrong.

"But let's get back to our job here. Let's take a look at those stab wounds. Hmm. Three entry points, all in the upper abdomen. We'll see what damage they did inside once I open her up."

When the abdomen was opened, it was full of blood. After this was carefully suctioned out, it was possible to trace the path of the three knife thrusts. Two penetrated the intestines multiple times. Those, the pathologist said, could easily be sutured, but the third wound entered the liver and sliced a large vein. "That one would have killed her, but I think it was the kick in the head that finished the job."

"What type of knife?"

"About six inches long with a narrow blade."

"Not a pen knife then."

"No."

"How would a guy bring that sort of knife with him? He couldn't carry it in his pocket."

"That's your problem, not mine. But off the record, I've seen a fisherman use a knife of about that size to gut fish, and it came in a sheath. Not a commercial fisherman. A guy fishing out here in the river. He carried it slung on his belt, but I suppose you could carry it in the pocket of a coat. I'm not saying the knife used here was of that type, just suggesting a possibility."

When the autopsy was finished, the pathologist summed up for Kalinski. "The order of the injuries: blow to the back of the neck, strangulation, knife wounds to the abdomen and face, then the kick in the head. She was not a virgin, but there was no sign of recent intercourse, nor any evidence that intercourse had been attempted. Time of death—late evening and before midnight. Rigor was fully established when Wynne Laird saw her this morning. By the way, her blood type was B, Rh positive, in case you need to match any blood splatters on a suspect's clothes."

Kalinski thanked him, and with a feeling of great relief, left the morgue.

CHAPTER TWENTY-ONE

The apartment house reeked of money. Al Rankin paused at the outer door, his hand hovering over the bell for number 602. He decided against ringing Clarice Packard directly. He rang for the manager, and when he got a response, he said, "This is Alan Rankin of the detective branch of the Centralia police force. I need to talk to a witness, and wanted to let you know beforehand that there will be no commotion and no arrest, which I'm sure you would like to be assured of. May I come in? I'll show you my credentials."

The door clicked open and Rankin entered and followed the signs showing the way to the manager's apartment. She stood in the hallway, watching him approach. He showed her his ID, which she scrutinized carefully. "Thank you," she said. "To whom do you want to speak?"

"I can't tell you that. It is very confidential."

The manager nodded and watched him leave and head for the elevator. He noted with relief that the elevator did not display the floor on which the cage stood, but only indicated that it was going either up or down. He wouldn't have to get off at the wrong floor and take the stairs to another floor in order to throw her off. He did not want her going to the phone to tip off Mrs. Packard. The elevator whisked him upward, letting him off at the sixth floor. The hallway was covered in thick, noise reducing carpet. The lighting was indirect, not too dim nor too bright. There were paintings on the walls. Luxury enveloped everything. Charles Packard must be shelling out a fortune if he is paying for this, Rankin thought.

He found number 602 and rang the bell, expecting to have to respond to a person who did not want to let him in. Instead, the door was thrown open and Clarice Packard stood there, an expression of surprise on her face. She appeared to be dressed for the street, not for lounging at home. He wondered who she had been expecting when she opened the door. She did not seem to be in a hurry and did not give him the tired old excuse of an urgent appointment.

"Who are you?" she challenged.

"Centralia Police Department," he said abruptly, walking through the door. "May I come in?"

"Since you're already in, it doesn't look as if I have much choice." She turned and led him into the living room, indicated a chair on one side of a low table and seated herself on the other side. She put a cigarette between her lips and leaned over to light it from an ornate lighter on the table. Seeing his hard stare, she remarked, "Charles wouldn't let me smoke in the house. He said he didn't want the children inhaling second-hand smoke. So now I'm out of that place, I can smoke whenever I want and I'm going to take advantage of it. Any objections?"

"It's your house," he stated equitably.

"So what do you want?"

"We are investigating the murder of your stepdaughter."

"What the hell do I care about what happened to that girl," Clarice Packard snarled. "She shouldn't have been out there walking the street at that time of night. I'm not surprised that she got herself killed."

Thinking that Clarice was suggesting that Dawn had been acting as a prostitute, Rankin grimaced in distaste. "She had a legitimate reason to be at the bus stop, and it wasn't all that late. Only about ten o'clock. So where were you at ten? Or let's say from nine to eleven last night."

"I was at home minding my own business."

"Do you mean here at this apartment, or the family home?"

"I live here. I've lived her ever since I left Charles. I'm done with those people for good. Her father could have the little slut for all I cared."

"Can anyone verify that you were here? Neighbors? Any friends call you?"

"No! I live by myself and plan to stay that way. You're not suggesting that I need an alibi or that I killed her, are you?"

"We are interviewing everyone who had any close contact with her. And you seem to be the one who disliked her the most."

"You can say that again. I couldn't stand her. She seemed like a nice little girl when I first met Charles, but after he conned me into marrying him, I found that at home she was a spoiled brat that I couldn't do anything with. And my son couldn't stand her, but she kept throwing insults at him.

It drove me crazy. I should never have married that guy. I'm filing for divorce and I'm going to get rid of that bunch for good."

You won't be able to live here if you do, Rankin thought. He was unable to get any more information out of her and rose to take his leave. "By the way, who was it that you were expecting when you opened the door?"

She threw back her head and laughed. "No one sinister. Just a friend I was going shopping with. She probably saw you at my door and decided to wait until you left. I'm going to go out and spend as much of Charles' money as I can."

And as he left, Rankin thought, And spend it before Charles cuts it off, which he will do once she files for divorce. He left the apartment privately hoping that she would turn out to be the one who had murdered the girl.

CHAPTER TWENTY-TWO

Keith Wall was staying at a downtown hotel, but was not in when Rankin called. Deciding to call Dawn Packard's lawyer, he hit pay dirt. Not only would Drew Robinson see him, but Keith Wall was there as well. When ushered into Robinson's office, he found the two men in friendly conversation and partaking of Robinson's office store of good whiskey. This was offered to Rankin, but he declined.

"I've closed the office for the rest of this week," the lawyer explained. "I was due to be in court anyway, and I've been hit hard by Dawn's murder. I had come to admire that young lady. She knew what she wanted and was dead set on getting it." He appeared drawn and tired, slumping in his chair. "Did you come to see me, or is it Keith you want to talk to?"

"I was looking for Mr. Wall."

"I'll leave you here in the office if you want to talk in private."

"Only if Mr. Wall wants it that way."

"I'm okay. There's nothing I mind Drew hearing."

So the lawyer and one of his witnesses had become chummy enough to be on a first name basis.

"How well did you know Dawn Packard?"

"I only met her once before, at the time my son died. I stayed a while to get everything sorted out; the funeral, the insurance. The insurance company said I'd never be able to get anything from the guy who ran my son off the road because he didn't die from his injuries. That's another place where I've lost out."

"I heard about that. It seems that Packard and his company lost out also. They couldn't collect on insurance policies, either. It seems that insurance companies consider euthanasia to be a type of suicide," Rankin remarked.

"They do." Robinson responded. "But that's not why the Packards couldn't claim on their policies. It's only when the insured person requests euthanasia, or consciously agrees to it, that it is regarded as a suicide. Brian was not able to make such a request..."

"And Brian wouldn't have, anyway, if he'd been conscious,"

Keith stated firmly.

"Yes. So that didn't enter into the decision by the insurance providers. It's the same as with Keith's claim. Brian didn't die from his injuries from the accident. The insurance provider assumes that Brian would have lived for thirty days. They won't accept any death that occurs any longer than that after the injury, thinking that the death might have been caused by something else," the lawyer explained. "They did pay out on the company's insurance policy, but not the double indemnity."

"Who was that paid to?" Rankin asked.

"Packard Electronics. It's a company policy, with the individual's consent, to protect them from loss of the key employees in the company."

"You seem to know a lot about it."

"This law firm has acted for the Packards for years. Those of us who have any dealings with the Packard family get together at intervals to pool information. We have a lot of specialists here. McNeill himself referred Dawn to me."

"I wonder, if euthanasia gets more common all over the country, whether the insurance companies will get together and come up with some way to deal with euthanasia, other than just denying claims," Rankin wanted to know.

"I doubt it. They will want to guard against someone who knows they're going to commit suicide or request euthanasia taking out a policy that will give their heirs a big payoff. They have reason to do so. Insurance fraud is a big problem for them."

"Yeah, I can see that. But won't it generally be an elderly person who is dying anyway…"

"Doesn't matter. They won't do it. Besides, in that case, the insurance company will think the heirs are pushing the old man to give up the ghost so they can collect on the policy."

"I've been a cop long enough to believe in that scenario. But let's get back to what you know about Dawn."

"I've corresponded with her about this case. I started thinking of her sort of as my daughter," Brian told the detective. "Packard called Brian his son, so why can't I call Dawn my daughter? I know it wouldn't work legally, but I never had a daughter and I lost my son. Clarice didn't want children and didn't expect to get pregnant, but I was delighted. But about Dawn, she was a spunky girl. I liked her.

I know her father better. While I was staying at his house, we talked a lot. I told him I was trying to save up enough to make a down payment on a larger building so I could expand. I operate a small-engine repair shop and wanted to get a franchise for a company that sells lawnmowers, snow blowers, chain saws, etc. But I had blown my savings on flying out here when I heard about my son's death. Packard told me to send him my business plan and he'd see if he could help me get a loan. He liked my plan, and he did co-sign a loan for me. I got the franchise and am doing well. I'm very grateful to him."

Robinson remarked, "I think part of it may have been from a feeling of guilt at not having told Keith when his son was injured. But he also saw good business sense in Keith's plans."

"He'll never have to spend a penny on his investment in my future. But you're right, he seemed flabbergasted when I told him no one had called me when Brian was hurt and no one asked my opinion on whether I wanted him killed. I don't blame Charles. I know he would have assumed that the hospital would have called me, or that Clarice would. Both of them should have."

"How old was Brian when you and your wife split up?"

"Thirteen."

"Why did she get custody when she didn't want children and you did, and your son was old enough to not need constant supervision?"

"I guess the judge was one of those who thought only a mother should have custody, and anyway, I was working ten hours a day, six days a week. But it was okay with me because I had access any time. Brian and I had a lot of fun together. Then Clarice got mad and out of spite moved clear out here.

I had to save up all year to be able to afford one trip for Brian to come back home for a visit, either at Christmas or spring break."

"I take it that Clarice didn't help pay for any of those trips, even though she was the one with money."

"No, she didn't. But once when Brian complained to Charles about it, he anteed up for a trip, and kept on doing so."

"Nice of him."

"Yeah, I thought so. Charles is a good guy. I don't know why he married Clarice. Have you met her?"

"I just finished talking to her."

"I bet you had to find her in a mall somewhere, spending money."

Rankin grinned. "I was lucky enough to find her at home, but she said she was just going out to do some shopping."

"She is in for a surprise. Packard told me he'd closed all their joint credit card accounts and their joint bank account."

"How can he do that without her consent?"

Robinson intervened. "The Charles Packards of this world have clout. And he is very chummy with the president of his bank. Furthermore, when she files for divorce, this firm has expert divorce attorneys as well."

Rankin turned back to Keith. "Does Mrs. Packard blame Dawn for breaking up her marriage?"

"You bet she does. She lets everyone know about it, too."

Robinson asked, "Are you thinking of that as a motive for murder?"

"As a long-time cop, I've seen many murders committed for far more trivial reasons than that."

"I would still have a hard time believing it."

"How about you, Mr. Wall?" But Keith only shrugged.

"I've got to ask this of everyone associated with Miss Packard. Where were you between nine and eleven last night?" Rankin asked.

"Right here."

"Here? In this office?"

"Yeah. Drew and I were going over my testimony for the next day, today in fact. I broke down while I was testifying yesterday and the cross examination was put off till today. The defense lawyers were set to have a go at me, and Drew was sort of putting me through my paces beforehand."

Rankin glanced at the lawyer, who replied. "That's correct. We were here in the office until ten at least, when we went down to the bar in the hotel across the street. We were there at least an hour."

"Were you a partner in the lawsuit, Mr. Wall?"

"No. Dawn asked me if I wanted to be, but I decided not. I told her I'd come and testify though. I planned to stay till the end of the trial to support her."

"Well, you seem to have the best possible alibi." Both the other men smiled. "But please do stay on, Mr. Wall. I'm asking that of all the people involved in this case."

Keith Wall snickered. "That snotty doctor who had to fly in from the coast isn't going to like it."

"Dr. Martin Schumacher, the great neurosurgeon," Robinson snorted, contempt in his voice. "He almost got the sack from his boss after he told the other doctors that Keith's son hadn't a chance to live, which gave the others, the ones who signed the approval forms, the justification they needed. But Dr. Bentley, the head neurosurgeon, said he thought Schumacher had learned his lesson and wouldn't make that mistake again, and it would be a shame to waste all those years of specialized training. I guess the guy probably has a guilt complex and is trying to hide it by pretending he is the best surgeon since the Mayo brothers.

"I looked up those guys when I was preparing this case. Schumacher finished his residency and got a position with a group of neurosurgeons over on the coast. He got married recently, his wife is very demanding, and he's seriously in debt. Professionally he's successful, but that wife of his spends every penny he makes.

"The other doctor, Mendel, is a contrast. Personally, an ordinary family man. Professionally, young for the responsibility he has, but highly respected by his peers."

Rankin commented, "From what I've heard about that case, Mendel seems to be the bad guy, but I understand that Miss Packard really had it in for the other one, Schumacher—along with her stepmother."

"That's right. Probably because he was the one she knew."

Rankin got up and stretched. "Anyway, we'll go talk to them and see what we think. Thanks for your time. You've both been very helpful."

CHAPTER TWENTY-THREE

The two detectives met at their office to review their afternoon's work. A pile of reports was also waiting. Kalinski picked up the top one and scanned it. "The house-to-house didn't come up with anything so far. Everyone seemed to be inside watching TV or getting ready for bed. No one saw or heard anything going on. But that jibes with the pathologist's findings. He thinks she was incapacitated by a blow to the back of the neck before she was choked, and there were no defensive injuries. He thought it unlikely that she'd have had a chance to cry out."

"A blow to the back of the neck? That's a new one to me."

"He showed me a bruise that he thought was from a karate chop."

"Anything else?"

"There were three stab wounds in the belly. One sliced a big vein and would have killed her, but he thought the kick in the head is what did it. A kick from a leather-soled shoe or boot." Kalinski went on to describe his other impressions of the autopsy, including the pathologist's thoughts about the knife. "He could have carried it in a large patch pocket, along with the raincoat. It was one of those temporary ones people take with them when they think it might rain before they get back. They come in a little packet and don't take much room. You can get them in dollar stores and drug stores."

Rankin nodded. "I know. Anything else?"

Kalinski picked up another report. "The weather people confirm what the bus driver told me. Rain started around a quarter after ten. The bus driver came down Hill Street on his last run a little after ten, but didn't see anything, but he was only looking for anyone who might be wanting to catch the bus. He couldn't say whether the body was lying there when he passed."

"If it'd been there, he'd have seen the yellow raincoat."

"I thought of that, but he might have just done the deed when he saw the bus coming and popped into the bushes until it passed. He'd be wearing the raincoat to keep from getting splashed with blood and he might not have taken it off yet."

"It could have happened that way. If not, it had to be right after the bus went by in order to get it all done before it started to rain. Did anyone get off the bus on its way up the street?"

"Two. But both were regular riders, known to the driver, and they went off in another direction."

"Okay. Anything from the phone company?"

Kalinski found the appropriate report and skimmed over it. "The call that got the girl to go out to the bus stop came from a pay phone at the mall."

"That figures. That's where the office for that petition campaign is located, and the guy said he was coming from there."

"He didn't come on the bus though."

"Maybe he had a car."

"So why wouldn't he drive around to her house?"

"Maybe he got a ride there."

"Could be. Dangerous for him, though. But I still think it's him. He could have gotten there on foot if he was young and healthy. The mall is only a block down from that pub, and the girl wouldn't have had to run over there to meet him."

"Don't close your mind to other possibilities," the older detective warned. "How about the obscene phone calls?"

"Made from another pay phone. This one over on the west side of town, from another mall over there, the West Hills Mall."

Rankin thought for a moment, then remarked, "That's where my dad lives. He still knows all the guys over there who have informers who give them tips. I think I'll ask him to pass the word around to ask about anyone who seems unusually upset about what the girl was doing. He'll enjoy doing it. He still misses the action."

"So what next?"

"Let's grab a bite, then go talk to those two doctors. I'll talk to Schumacher and you take Mendel. Tomorrow morning, I think we need another talk with the Packards, both the father and the aunt. We also need to get the poison pen letter from the aunt and ask about boyfriends. I'll go over to my dad's for breakfast and get him on the job over there. And send someone to go to the newspaper and get the addresses of the nasty letter writers. I don't expect much, but let's not overlook them."

CHAPTER TWENTY-FOUR

Dr. Martin Schumacher was not pleased when Rankin tracked him down in the bar at his hotel.

"We can talk here or go to your room, whichever you like."

Schumacher sighed and slid off the barstool. Silently, he led the way to the elevator and took Rankin to his room. "So what do you want?"

"We would like to know where you were between nine o'clock and midnight last night."

"Why?"

"We think the murder was committed during that time period."

"What murder?"

"You must have known about it. It caused your trial to be cancelled."

"All I know is that the plaintiff didn't turn up and I came all this way for nothing."

"Come on! You're not that dumb. You must have known why she didn't show up. So where were you between nine o'clock and midnight last night?"

"If it's any of your business, I was right here."

"In this room?"

Schumacher nodded.

"All the time? Come on, I've already talked to the bartender who was on last night." Rankin hadn't, but he thought that the bar was probably where the man had been, and decided to take a chance.

"All right. So I was there. If you talked to the bartender, he will have told you that, so why ask me?"

"Getting up a little courage for your ordeal today?"

"I was watching a basketball game on the TV."

"Not on the TV in your room?"

"So what?"

"Who was playing?"

"The Lakers and the Celtics."

"Who won?"

"The Celtics. Do you want to know the score?"

"When you left the bar, did you go directly back to your room?"

"Yes."

The answer was given firmly with no hesitation. He had probably gone back to his room when he left the bar, but could he have made a side trip out to Hill Street before he went to the bar? Rankin wanted to rattle this supercilious excuse for a man. "Did you know that your patient's biological father wasn't told that his son was in the hospital with serious injuries?"

"Why should I know?"

"He was your patient."

"Yeah, and the family was there all the time with that girl always getting in the way."

"Didn't you think your patient's father should have been asked his opinion on euthanasia?"

"He wasn't there, so how could we ask him?"

"He wasn't there because nobody told him."

"Well, that's not my problem."

Rankin gave up. "You will have to remain in town until we tell you that you can leave."

Schumacher jumped to his feet. "Look here, I'm a busy man. I had to cancel a lot of patients in order to come here. I've got to go back."

"The world won't come to an end in the next day or two if you have to stay here."

"You can't order me around like that. I'm an important surgeon."

"As a matter of fact, we can order you. Solving this crime is even more important."

Schumacher sighed, the defiance draining out of his face. "Why can't you leave me alone?" he asked petulantly.

CHAPTER TWENTY-FIVE

Dr. Steve Mendel was a polar opposite to the cranky surgeon. For once, when he opened the door to Kalinski at about eight o'clock that night, he was not wearing surgical scrubs. Instead he was clad in jeans and a T-shirt. He led Kalinski into the living room. The place was strewn with toys and video games while four children created a blur of motion. A baby who had reached the crawling stage was navigating with amazing speed across the room, followed by a boy of about seven or eight, keeping watch on the baby. Two other children of intermediate age, a boy and a girl, were quarreling over a toy. Mrs. Mendel stuck her head through the door from the kitchen and yelled, "Let your sister have it. She had it first." The boy reluctantly gave up the toy.

"I understand that you are investigating the murder of the Packard girl. I don't know what I can do to help, but I'll do whatever I can," the surgeon said. "A girl that young being murdered is a real tragedy. So much potential there, now lost."

"We are interviewing everyone who had any contact with Miss Packard. That includes the defendants in the lawsuit she filed."

Mendel smiled. "Ah. So I'm a suspect am I? That's a novel idea to me. But fire away."

"Where were you last night?"

Mendel waved his hand over the room and grimaced. "Here!"

Kalinski had to laugh and the doctor joined him.

"And besides, the baby is teething and we were up all night with her."

Mrs. Mendel entered carrying a tray containing a variety of home-baked cookies and a pot of coffee, milk and sugar. "You look like you've been working too hard and probably haven't had much time to eat."

Kalinski hesitated, but Mendel smiled and said, "Doctor's orders. Joanie is a great cook. I don't know how she can keep up with the monsters and still have time to come up with great meals and all kinds of goodies." Kalinski sank into a comfortable chair and let himself be plied with coffee and cookies. After serving the two men, Mrs. Mendel seated herself beside her husband.

"How well did you know Miss Packard?"

"I didn't really know her at all. She was there at the hospital the last time I talked to the family about donating the young man's organs. I felt sorry for her. She was desperately anxious that her brother—or I guess he was her stepbrother—should live. According to Martin Schumacher, there was really no chance of that. I hadn't expected such a reaction. I had only previously talked to the mother and stepfather."

"I think the debate is over whether he should have been given more time to see if he would regain consciousness," Kalinski observed.

Mendel leaned forward, his forearms resting on his knees, staring at the floor. His wife put her hand over his and gave it a squeeze. He glanced at her and a small, tender smile passed between them. Stan Kalinski had the impression that the two were still deeply in love. Mendel did not answer the detective's implied question, and Kalinski let it go. Instead, he asked, "Were you able to transplant all the organs you took from him?"

"Yes. We are a regional hospital for organ transplanting in this part of the country. We had two kidney patients right here in Centralia who got his kidneys. So far, they are doing as well as can be expected. You have to realize that these are very sick people, and the transplanted organ is not a miracle cure. They also have to be treated with drugs to prevent the donated organ from being rejected. The drugs suppress their immune system so that it doesn't attack the foreign organ. But that also means that they are more susceptible to infections. They will never be normal, but their lives are vastly better and they aren't on the verge of immediate death."

While he was talking, the little girl came over with her toy. "It broke," she said. Mendel reached out and took the toy, snapped the loose piece back into place and returned it to the child, who ran away happily. All this while continuing with his narrative without a hitch.

"The other organs went to patients at other hospitals. There is a nationwide registry. I don't know how those donations turned out. His corneas were banked. They don't have to be immediately transplanted. One of these days we will be able to take stem cells from the patient and get them to grow into the organ that is needed, without the rejection factor, but it will be a few years yet before that is practical.

"You have to realize how frustrating it is to go in every day and see patients, all of them on the edge of death, pleading, begging, threatening and even trying to bribe me to find them the organ they need before they die while waiting. I have to keep telling them that we haven't had a suitable organ donated, and as much as I'd like to help them, I can't."

"Yes, it must be frustrating," Kalinski responded.

Joan Mendel leaned forward. "You know, it's not as if he's trying to get the family of every accident victim to agree to euthanasia so their organs can be harvested. This was a one off." The surgeon did not respond to this, but sat staring at the floor.

Kalinski asked, "If your work is so stressful, how can you come home to all these kids and all this chaos?"

"Actually, I find it relaxing. As I told you, I spend my days with people who are dying, and to come home to this explosion of vibrant life makes all my tenseness melt away. I love it."

Kalinski found himself liking this man, but he had to ask a question he knew would be troubling.

"Did you know that Brian Wall's biological father was not notified that he was in the hospital and was not asked whether he agreed to euthanasia?"

Mendel jerked his head up and stared at the detective. "No. I didn't. Are you sure?" There was a gasp from Joan Mendel.

"Yes, I'm sure. Didn't you hear him testify yesterday afternoon?"

"I was only there in the morning. I couldn't get away all day. I didn't hear that."

The older boy, who had been sitting cross-legged beside the baby, who was now asleep in the middle of the floor, got up and came over to his father, leaning against the man's thigh. "What's the matter, Dad?"

"It's okay Jack. I just heard something disturbing. Just keep an eye on Sarah, will you? Thanks Jack."

The boy went away after giving Kalinski a questioning glance. Mendel watched his son then turned back to face Kalinski.

"No, I didn't know that. That's awful. If I'd known, I certainly would have expected him to voice his opinion."

"But you knew that Brian Wall was Packard's stepson."

"I'm not sure I took that in. I can't remember whether I did know at the time. I do now." There was a hint of bitterness in his voice as he said the last.

When Kalinski rose to leave, Joan Mendel followed him to the door. "I'm sure you discount a wife's evidence that gives her husband an alibi, but Steve really was here all last night."

"We don't always expect it not to be accurate, but we do run into cases where the wife will lie her head off to save her husband." Mrs. Mendel smiled, but said no more and Kalinski went on. "Then there are times when we truly believe the wife. Good night, and thank your husband for me for being so forthright.

CHAPTER TWENTY-SIX

Rankin stretched and set down his empty coffee cup. "I hope your visit last night went better than mine. I seem to have gotten the stinkers."

"I would have traded you my autopsy for your Clarice Packard."

"No thanks. How did it go with the evil Dr. Mendel?"

"He's not so evil. I really liked him, and I'm sure he was at home last night." Kalinski described his visit, including Mendel's explanation of why he liked to come home to the vibrant chaos that was his family. "I got the impression that whenever things got really tough at work, he'd come home to his lovely wife and make another baby."

Rankin roared with laughter. "Hey, guy. You need to find a girl you can go to when you're uptight and make a baby yourself. Or do you have some young woman waiting for you to finish this case right now?"

Stan Kalinski turned red with embarrassment, and seeing his younger companion's discomfort, Rankin changed the subject.

"I think the first thing for us to do this morning is to revisit the Packards. They'll know who she was dating."

Kalinski reached for the phone and dialed the Packard home. "I'm going to be busy for the next couple of hours," Charles told them. "I haven't been to the office, and there are some things that need my attention, so my secretary is bringing them over and we'll work here. I should be done by ten thirty if that's all right with you."

"That would be fine, Mr. Packard."

A call to Dr. Madge Packard elicited the information that she would be out at a meeting at the U. during the afternoon, but if they could come right over, she would be available. They would be there in twenty minutes, Kalinski told her.

Madge Packard let them into the house, led them into an expertly furnished living room and offered coffee. Stan Kalinski realized he hadn't really noticed the house the previous morning when they had been there, and kicked himself for what he considered a dereliction of duty for not paying attention to his surroundings. Now he surveyed the arrangement of the furniture into groupings that met the needs for various activities. It was a large room. One area was obviously arranged for intimate conversation between the hostess and her guests, another group made a semicircle around the TV, which was set in a corner, while another was based on an expensive hi-fi set. Classical music was playing, and Madge Packard went to the console to turn down the volume, leaving it as background music. No rock and roll here, Stan thought. The colors in the room were muted pastels with bright accents. Paintings were highlighted by indirect lighting.

Rankin got right down to business.

"What did you think of your niece's program to try to get the law on euthanasia changed?"

"I had originally been in favor of decriminalizing euthanasia. But I had to admit that I hadn't thought that it could be used to do something like they did to Brian. He was a fine young man, and I think they should have waited longer before they gave up on him. I still think that older people who haven't much to live for, or people with those devastating degenerative diseases should be allowed to end their own life or have someone do it for them."

"What about the argument that his healthy organs could be transplanted into other people and save their lives?"

"That is the only good thing that came out of it. But they should have waited longer."

"Did you try to talk Miss Packard out of going on with her campaign?"

"No. It was her opinion, and she had a right to it." The professor was obviously in tune with the feeling of academics everywhere that freedom of speech should be upheld, even if it was unpopular.

"So there was no bad feeling between you?"

"None at all. I loved that girl. I was very happy to have her come live with me. The atmosphere in her home was becoming downright poisonous."

"You don't like your sister-in-law?"

"Charles should never have married that woman."

"Why did he?"

"He had just lost his first wife, Dawn's mother, to breast cancer. He loved her very much and was devastated by her death. We are what are known as 'cultural Christians', in fact more nearly 'cultural Anglicans', people who come from an English background whose basic church affinity was with the Church of England, called Episcopalians in the United States. Locally, we are what are called C and E members, those who go to church at Christmas and Easter. However, in Charles' bereavement, he started attending church regularly. The priest at the time was very helpful in guiding Charles through the grief process."

"I thought priests were all Catholic," Rankin interjected.

"No. Our church has priests also. Our current one is Reverend Clifton James, a fine man, very scholarly."

"Sorry to interrupt. Go on."

"In church, he met a woman of his age with a teenage son she was raising on her own. She said nothing about a divorce, and I think Charles assumed that she was a widow. He liked the boy, who was dragged to church every Sunday. She made a play for Charles, because of his wealth, I'm sure. His resistance was weak. He thought Dawn should have a mother figure in the house." Madge paused for a moment, then remarked with feeling, "He should have hired a governess."

"Did the new Mrs. Packard make a good mother for Dawn?"

"She did NOT."

"How did the girl react to the new stepmother?"

"They never did get along. Charles let Dawn have a good deal of freedom, though he did have rules, but Clarice's view was that children should be neither seen nor heard.

134

Dawn had a room full of toys and games, and a few books. Clarice made her stay in that room unless she had a chore for the girl to do, or at mealtime. In the summer, she was allowed in the back yard, but not the garden, where previously Dawn had her own little patch to grow her own garden. The hired gardener defied Clarice and let Dawn help him."

"When did the marriage start to break up?"

"I know that Charles was unhappy almost from the start, but I guess their relationship began to deteriorate when Brian developed an interest in the things Charles did, and Charles encouraged him. Charles often took Brian to work with him, and would give him a guide, so to speak, to show him around the plant. In the evenings, he and Brian spent hours together, and the boy was encouraged to take science courses. I guess you know that Brian studied electrical engineering, Charles' field, at the University and was expected to step into a good job at Packard Electronics. Clarice seemed to feel that Charles had deliberately stolen him away from her."

"What plans had she had for her son?"

"I have no idea, if she had any at all."

"What caused Mrs. Packard to decide to move out?"

"It was when Dawn went to that lawyer and instructed him to file suit against everyone who had been responsible for Brian's euthanasia, and that of course, included Clarice."

"Did Dawn move in with you right away?"

"That very day!"

"Now, let's talk about Dawn's boyfriends. Who were the serious ones? Any steady boyfriend for a period of time?"

"She always had dates, ever since she reached puberty. You may not have known it, only seeing her after she was dead, but she was a very pretty girl. She was popular. The boys more or less lined up. But the last year and a half of high school, Jon Smits was her steady boyfriend. His father is a trust officer at our bank."

That made him eminently respectable, in the Packard mindset, Kalinski thought.

"A nice boy. I liked him, and so did Charles."

"Do you know his address? We would like to talk to him."

"You will have trouble doing so at this time."

"Why?"

"At the end of the school year, last summer, he left for Europe. He planned to spend a gap year traveling around Europe. He asked Dawn to go with him, but she turned him down because of this lawsuit coming up."

"How did he feel about that?"

"I think he was a bit put out. I think they had a quarrel just before he left. I was sorry about that, but could only let them settle their own differences." Madge paused for a minute, frowning, as if deciding whether to tell them something she would rather keep quiet about. "I think I should tell you, I have the feeling that Dawn probably had sex with this boy. I haven't told Charles. The reason I think so is that she came home late one evening trying to hide some sort of excitement, and rather avoided me as she went to her room. And I think her demeanor when she was with Jon changed. They seemed more intimate."

"Did that bother you?"

"Not really. You have to expect that with young people these days don't you? And if she were going to have sex with anyone, I would prefer that it be a young man like Jon. Still, I was hesitant to tell Charles, and decided not to."

To the detectives, this revelation was no surprise. It confirmed the pathologist's report.

"Do you know definitely that he's in Europe?"

"The last e-mail Dawn got from him, he said he was in Davos, Switzerland and planned to do some skiing."

"How long ago was that?"

"Sometime last week, I think. We can look it up. I haven't even turned on her computer. She might have deleted the e-mail, but I think she saved those from Jon."

They trekked upstairs to Dawn's bedroom and found her laptop sitting on her desk. Opening it, Madge checked the girl's e-mail and found the one from Jon in Davos. "He used to send twitters, or do you call them tweets? I have never gotten into that myself, so don't know how to do it. I don't know whether things like that get saved on her phone."

"If you will let us, we can check the phone and find out. Do you know where it is? She didn't have it on her when we inventoried the contents of her pockets, nor was it found at the site."

"She may not have taken it with her, since she didn't know the person she went to meet. I think it's downstairs on the kitchen counter."

"Let's check the computer first." They found a list of past e-mails from Jon sent, he said, from places starting in London and continuing through France and Germany, before ending in Switzerland. They were long, newsy letters describing his travels. They had come every two or three days, but the most recent had been sent eight days before her death.

"Dawn was a bit upset that she hadn't heard from him for so long."

"There are several other people who received this e-mail," Kalinski observed. "Do you know whether any of the others got e-mails since this one?"

"I have no idea."

"May we take this computer with us? You will get it back when we're through with it."

"Of course."

"We can't rule him out," Rankin commented to Kalinski as Madge went ahead of them to search for Dawn's cell phone. "An e-mail can be sent from anywhere and eight days is plenty of time for him to get home."

After turning the cell phone over to the policemen, Madge led them back to the living room. "What else do you want to know?"

"We were talking about boyfriends. Any others?"

"Oh yes, that's what we were talking about." She refilled their cups from the coffee pot she had brought with her from the kitchen.

Madge went on, "Last summer, she dated another boy from her high school class a few times. His name is Dave Brewster and he's now at the University, but I think he still lives at home. Dawn broke off with him when he got extremely jealous of her talking to another man. I think it must have been from her continuing to correspond with Jon. Dawn told Dave that she was not his property and he had no right to tell her whom she could talk to."

"You don't think she had sex with Brewster?"

"Oh, no. Not at all. He was a more casual boyfriend, at least as far as Dawn was concerned."

"Any others?"

"I don't know whether you can consider Alex Hamilton as a boyfriend, or whether her relationship with him was pure business. When he heard that she was starting this petition drive, he came over one day and offered his help. He has turned the drive into something big that can't be ignored."

"We've heard about him. How well do you know him?"

"He was older. He went to the same school, but had graduated before Dawn started." She thought for a minute. "I can't think of any others."

"We would like to get in touch with these kids who were on Smits' mailing list, and any others who were close friends of Miss Packard. Do you have any idea how we can get them all together?"

"Hmmm. Let me think. I could call Margo Cunningham. She is a close friend of mine and her daughter, Lindsey, was one of Dawn's best friends." Suiting the action to the words, she reached for the phone. After the exchange of pleasantries, much of which had to do with laments of Dawn's death, the two women got down to business. Words such as Saturday noon and pizza were used, and when Madge put down the phone, she had the plan all worked out. Mrs. Cunningham would have her daughter get all the other youths together to meet at the Cunningham home the next day, Saturday, at noon for a pizza party. "Bring your appetites, both of you. The kids, she thinks, will be more than willing to come. They are all pretty upset by the murder, and want to help. Prepare to have your ears talked off."

CHAPTER TWENTY-SEVEN

Charles Packard was finishing his work with his secretary when the detectives arrived. "I'll finish typing up these letters while you talk to the policemen, and you can sign them before I leave," the secretary, a smartly dressed middle-aged woman, told him.

"Will it bother you if we stay in here?" Charles asked his secretary.

"Not at all. But leave me access to the printer." She had been typing on her laptop, perched on the edge of Charles' desk.

He waived the two policemen to chairs and turned toward them. His shoulders drooped and he seemed tired. He was clad in slacks, an open-necked shirt and slippers. Kalinski wondered whether the man had been able to get any sleep.

"How can I help you?" Packard asked.

"We wanted to know about any boyfriends Dawn had in the last two or three years. Did Dawn keep in touch with you when she moved in with Dr. Packard, or could there be any friends she didn't tell you about?"

"We saw each other nearly daily. She would drop in at the plant on her way home from school. We remained very close."

"Did she tell you about her dates with boys?"

"If she was serious about them, she would. She was very enthusiastic about a boy named Jon Smits, one of her high school classmates. But he left for Europe last summer. I think she still got e-mails from him."

"She did. They were still on her computer. Did she say anything to you about a quarrel with him before he left?"

"No, she didn't. It must not have been a serious one. I think she would have told me if it had been. I took an interest in my daughter. Probably if her mother had been alive, she would have been the one Dawn brought her troubles to, but I have become both her mother and her father since my wife's death. I have been very close to my daughter."

"Did this cause any problems between you and your current wife?"

Charles sighed, and there was sadness in his voice as he said, "Yes it did. Unfortunately, my wife and my daughter did not get along well. I think Clarice resented the attention I gave to Dawn, but she was my daughter. What could I do?"

"Was she dating other boys while she was going out with Smits?"

"No."

"After he left, was she?"

"Yes, she was. There were several. She was popular. But the only one she went out with more than once was another high school classmate, Dave Brewster."

"For how long?"

"Not long. It seems that he got very possessive and Dawn resented that and told him off. I don't think she considered him more than a boy it was fun to go out with occasionally."

"Do you know specifically what it was that caused her to break off with him?"

"No, I don't."

"Anyone else?"

"I don't know whether you can call Alex Hamilton a boyfriend or not. He is the young man who is helping her with the petition campaign. He is in his last year of an MBA course at the University. He must be in his mid-twenties. Really nice young man. We know his family. His father and I are on the boards of several charities. We also see them at the Symphony. Nice people. I wouldn't have minded at all if Dawn had gotten serious about him. He did take her out, to dinner and then a concert, a time or two. I can't think of any others."

The secretary was standing at Charles' shoulder with the letters for him to sign. As he reached for them, she said, "How about that boy you hired last summer who was always pestering your daughter, until she went out to lunch with him one time?"

Charles snorted. "Not really a boyfriend." To the detectives he explained, "Dawn had enough experience that I put her in charge of the order department while the regular person was on maternity leave. She took orders, listed the things that need to be pulled off the shelf, checked that the correct ones were pulled and sent to the mailroom. Kyle Quigley got a job last summer as one of the gofers who gather the items and brought them to Dawn for checking. Regular little nuisance, and we finally had to let him go.

Always hanging around Dawn, wanting to get help or advice from her. At first she helped him and even went with him one day to some fast food place for a burger. She expected to pay for hers, but the kid insisted on paying. Dawn realized that he considered it a date and wanted to be her boyfriend, so she never agreed to go out with him again. But he kept pestering her at work until she finally told him she didn't have time to hold his hand."

The secretary remarked, "It was just puppy love on his part. Dawn had no interest in him, but he kept after her because it gave him a chance to be with her."

"He didn't give up after he left the company. He came to Dawn's petition office one night, but when he found that he was expected to work, he left. Dawn told me about it. And she told me that one day, he came to Madge's house, but stopped out on the street when he saw her car coming. She drove on in without acknowledging his presence and he left. No, I certainly wouldn't call him a boyfriend."

"Maybe he's the one Dave Brewster saw her with and got so jealous."

"It could have been."

Kalinski asked, "Mr. Packard, what was your opinion of your daughter's program to overturn the euthanasia law?"

"I agree with it after what they did to my stepson. I would never have tried to stop her. If you want some sound reasons why, talk to Alex Hamilton. He'll give you some well thought out argument as to why it's a bad law."

When the detectives left, Kalinski commented, "She was pretty hard on her boyfriends."

"Yeah, didn't take any guff from them. Toe the line or you're gone."

"I wonder if Brewster held a grudge."

"Could be. Let's go find out."

CHAPTER TWENTY-EIGHT

The Brewster home was in an older section of town, closer to the city center. The houses were from an immediate post World War II era, many lived in by families where a returning serviceman had used his veteran's rights to buy a home for his new family, some having bequeathed the property to one of their children. A well-tended yard with flowerbeds surrounded the Brewster house. There were window baskets, now empty of flowers. Brewster senior managed a store in a national chain of tire stores, while Mrs. Brewster served as a secretary at one of the elementary schools. The policemen had researched these things before coming. Quietly comfortable, but not wealthy, was Kalinski's analysis.

Brewster lived in a room off the basement of his parents' house. Entry was by way of the large basement room, which was full of gym equipment.

"Body builder?" Rankin asked, noticing the young man's broad shoulders, bull neck and bulging biceps beneath a tight-fitting T-shirt. "Or football player?"

"Yeah. Both when I was in high school. Not now. I just like to keep in shape. Dad uses the equipment, too, though he doesn't need to. He's in pretty good shape for a guy who's nearly fifty. I work for him weekends, changing tires." He grinned. "That helps build the muscles." He led them into his room and sat on the bed. Rankin took the only chair, a desk chair beside a student's desk, and Kalinski leaned against the doorframe.

Kalinski asked, "Did you go to Baker High?"

"Yeah, I did. I'm at the U. now."

"What position?"

"Defensive tackle. You look like you might have played football too."

"Centralia High. Offensive line, either tackle or guard. I played for three years."

Brewster gave him a barely visible smile, along with what appeared to Kalinski to be a supercilious expression. He longed to put this guy in his place by pointing out that Centralia, the oldest high school in town, had routinely thrashed the rich kids from Edmund Baker, once by a score of 56 to 7. But after a quick glance at Rankin, he chose to keep his mouth shut. He asked, "Any other sports?"

"Oh, yeah. I've tried a lot of them, but I like football best. We had a phys ed teacher in high school who thought we ought to try out various sports, so he gave us a week on each of them. He was a karate fanatic. I thought it was pretty silly. I like boxing, and if one of those guys ever aimed a kick at my head, I'd just step inside it and clock him with a left hook and put him flat on his back listening to tweety birds."

"Ever try it?"

"Nah! Never had a chance. What do you guys want?"

"You used to date Dawn Packard, didn't you?" Rankin asked.

"A couple of times. Shitty rich bitch, if you want to know."

"I hear she told you off."

"That type of broad thinks she owns the earth."

"You still hold a grudge?"

Brewster shrugged. "She's old news. I've got other girls I like better."

"You aren't sorry that she got murdered?"

He shrugged and said nothing.

"Did she involve you in her petition campaign?"

"She tried to, but I wasn't interested. I couldn't have cared less."

"Where were you Wednesday night?"

"Here. Studying. We had exams all week."

"You didn't go out at all?"

"No."

And he maintained that assertion consistently as they tried to break down his calm denial.

"No alibi," Kalinski commented as they walked back to their car. "And doesn't seem to care."

"We may have to take him in, where he's not so sure of himself, and shake him down a bit. Big brute of a guy—could easily do all those things to the girl. But we still have to talk to the newer boyfriend. Let's go see what Alexander the Great Hamilton has to say for himself."

CHAPTER TWENTY-NINE

The detectives were admitted to the Hamilton home by the housekeeper and ushered into an elegantly furnished drawing room where Alex Hamilton and his parents were waiting for them. Classical music was playing in the background. The elder Hamilton rose and came to meet them, shaking hands with both men. "Horrible thing, this murder," he said. "I hope you find the person who did it quickly."

"We are trying to," Rankin replied. "We hope your son can help."

The younger man nodded and stepped forward. "I'll do anything I can to help."

He was a tall, well-built young man, graceful in his movements, dressed in brown cords, a plaid shirt and matching cashmere sweater. He brushed his wavy dark brown hair back from his forehead and regarded the detectives with steady gray eyes. Kalinski though he had probably not slept well. He had a sort of gray look about him.

"Dad said we could use his den to talk." He turned and led them into a typically masculine room with large leather chairs, pine paneling half way up the wall and racing prints above.

"Your father must be a horse racing fan," Rankin remarked.

"We own a racehorse. He's called Shining Armour."

"Does it win?"

Alex smiled. "Enough to pay the training fees."

"Do you bet on your horse?"

"No. Dad is the CEO of one of the country's leading investment firms. He is very knowledgeable about risk-taking in financial matters. He thinks gambling of any sort is a waste of money. We go to the races because we love to watch the horses. They are such beautiful animals." He grinned and added, "But if our horse was a Derby winner, we'd probably bet on it."

"Okay, let's get this out of the way first. Where were you on Wednesday night?"

"Here at home, studying. I had a couple of big exams coming up."

"Can anyone verify that?"

"My folks came upstairs to bed around ten thirty. Dad stuck his head in my door and said good night. Other than that, no. It's a big house and the garage is at the opposite end from the bedrooms, so I could have sneaked out."

"Did you?"

"No." It was said with a smile. "I know you think of family and close friends first, but we all liked Dawn. I would never have hurt a hair on her head."

"Do any of the servants live in the house?"

"We call them employees, not servants. But no, none of them live here."

"Okay. There's something else we want to know, to get the background on this case. We are told that you can tell us what's behind this campaign that Dawn Packard was waging. Why was it so important?"

"I think that's self-evident. You know about Dawn's stepbrother being...being killed, to put it bluntly." Rankin nodded and Alex went on. "It was important to get the law changed so that sort of thing would never happen again."

"In spite of the fact that for a lot of people it would be a boon to get over the misery at the end of their lives."

"My personal opinion was that it was unlikely that the law would be entirely repealed, but that if enough attention was given to the horrible mistakes that could be made, like Brian's death, that more safeguards would be put in place. I had read up on the information a leading medical ethicist has presented on that subject. She says that in the Netherlands, where euthanasia has been in effect for years, there has been a slide toward euthanasia for convenience, and that people who do it do indeed become hardened. She relates one case where a Down's Syndrome child, who was otherwise healthy, was put down. That amounts to making a judgment about the value of life that doesn't recognize the preciousness of human life, that doesn't recognize the human soul."

"I see your point. But what makes you so personally involved?"

"You didn't meet my grandmother, but she lives here with us. She is deathly afraid to go to a nursing home because she thinks that people will think that she is merely a frail old lady who is taking up a bed and ought to be gotten rid of to make room for a younger, more useful person. We have all tried to reassure her that we would never agree to that, but she still thinks that the staff might make that decision and do it without telling us about it. Since the new law came in, she has been even more frightened. She thinks that when hospital staff get used to euthanizing people, they will lose their ability to question whether it is right, and be more willing to do it. She is afraid of the kind of people who work with the aged and think they are useless and decide to slip some deadly drug into them. It happens every once in a while."

"It happened before euthanasia became legal."

"Yes, but she thinks they would become more bold about doing it if they thought it was legal anyway. That's her way of thinking. I'm not sure she's right, but it causes her a great deal of anguish. Fortunately we can care for her at home. She has a nurse with her during the day and we can care for her at night. Mother is very good with her, and gives my grandmother some peace of mind. But one of these days, my grandmother will have to go to the hospital for some reason, and is still afraid of what will happen to her."

He leaned forward, rested his forearms on his knees and continued, "I recognize that there are many people who are at the end of life and have no hope for the future, who would find it a relief to be able to get the experience of dying over with as soon as possible. But also, they may make this decision at a time when they are feeling very low, and then in a day or two their treatment will go into effect and they will feel better."

"There's a waiting period for that reason. It gives people a chance to change their mind," Kalinski commented.

Alex nodded. "That is a good clause in the current law. But what really needs to be done is to develop more palliative care places, and to put more stress on palliative care. I think one of the problems is that doctors are afraid to give patients adequate pain relief because they might get themselves into trouble with the law. High doses of narcotics could shorten the person's life. There needs to be a provision in the law that says that if the intent was only to relieve pain and not to hasten death, it should be acceptable. Also, some authorities might also claim that giving high doses of narcotics can cause addiction, but if the patient is only going to live for days, or even weeks anyway, why worry about addiction? Doctors know that, but lay people often don't. And I've heard that if you really need narcotics to control your pain, you won't become addicted to them, no matter how much you need to take.

"Then there's also the question of family members trying to hurry an old person into the grave. I don't know just how to deal with that, other than to repeal the law.

"I also heard from Dawn that insurance companies won't pay on a policy when the person agrees to euthanasia, because they consider it a form of suicide. I can imagine some old person agreeing to euthanasia in order that their children can inherit their estate more quickly, before it is all used up in medical bills, only to have the part that wasn't used to pay the bills, the insurance, denied so they get nothing anyway.

"Am I making myself clear?"

"Absolutely," Kalinski murmured.

Rankin scratched his head. "We heard that you were the one to explain this to us. I guess they were right. Did you and Dawn agree on this?"

"Well, not completely. She was more interested in getting revenge for the death of her brother. But she said that anything she got in a settlement in the court case would be given to the local hospice."

"Did you believe her?"

"Yes, I did."

"Did you and she get along well?"

Alex hesitated before he answered. "You might as well know that she could be pretty demanding about getting her way if you didn't agree with her. But when it came to how to run the campaign, she recognized that what I was doing worked a lot better than what she'd been doing before, so we could work together all right."

"We've been told that you took her out to dinner and to concerts."

"Once. My dad is a member of the board of directors of the Symphony. So is Mr. Packard. Ever since I've been old enough, I've been expected to turn up at the Symphony gala each fall, with an appropriate young lady. I'm not trying to brag, only giving you information, but I'm considered to be one of Centralia's most eligible bachelors. But I got so busy this year, I almost forgot, and I had to find someone in a hurry. Dawn knows what it's all about, I knew she would have an appropriate ball gown to wear, and I knew she wouldn't embarrass me by comparing the soloist with her favorite rock star, so I asked her. There's a concert in late afternoon and a formal dinner after."

"But let's get back to Wednesday night. Did you send one of your volunteers to meet Miss Packard at that bus stop in order to get a letter signed?"

"Did I do what?"

"Miss Packard was lured out to that bus stop by someone who said you had a letter that she needed to sign, and had sent the person who called up there to meet her."

"I did no such thing." Alex was sitting bolt upright. "Look! If I had needed a letter signed, I would have taken it over to Dawn's house."

"Would any of your volunteers have done so?"

"No. We weren't even working that night. As I told you, it's exam week, and most of us are students. You aren't thinking of interviewing all of them are you?"

"If we need to."

"Well, good luck. There are dozens, if not hundreds."

The housekeeper let the detectives out, but not before she admonished them. "Now don't you go giving Alex a bad time. He's a fine boy, and don't you forget it!"

CHAPTER THIRTY

As they got back into their car, Kalinski remarked. "An MBA degree is wasted on that lad. He should be studying psychology or law or something like that."

Rankin grunted. "I guess everyone was right about him being the one to go to about this euthanasia deal."

Back at their office, Kalinski picked up a bunch of reports that had been piling up on his desk. He began to read them over.

"Here's the forensic stuff. There was some bloody water trapped in a fold of the raincoat. Type B, Rh positive; the girl's blood type. No other blood unless it was the same type. They found a few threads on the inside of a sleeve, in case we find a coat or shirt to compare them with. Dark blue. The raincoat was one of those throwaway things that you can buy at a game if it looks like it's going to rain before you go home. They come in a little pouch you can carry in your pocket." He read on. "We should be looking for shoes or boots with a leather sole. It might have picked up some blood or skin."

"Unless it's been discarded like the knife."

"Yeah." Kalinski picked up another report and read for a while. "Here's the signed statement from the bus driver on that route. He says he let two people off at the stop on the other side of the street and several more between there and the end of the route at the hospital. He turns around there and comes back down. He didn't pick up anyone at the stop where the murder took place. Says he only glanced at the bus stop to see if anyone was waiting for the bus. Wouldn't have noticed a body behind the bench or anyone walking down the street. His next stop is at the mall. It's a timed stop. He can't leave until ten twelve. He says it was sprinkling when he pulled out and started to rain hard two or three minutes later. He picked up a bunch of hockey fans there. There's an arena where they have recreational league games. No change from what he told me."

"Good. That gives us bookends for the time of the murder. And it agrees with the pathologist's time of death."

"Nothing useful from the house-to-house. No one noticed anyone waiting there, no strange cars parked on the street, and they didn't hear anything. There wouldn't have been anything to hear. The pathologist said the assailant first incapacitated the girl with a karate type chop to the back of the neck. He said it was the first injury because there was time for bruising to develop before she died. He thinks she was throttled next, enough to fracture her hyoid bone, but not kill her. Done from in front. She was stabbed next, three times in the abdomen, not the chest, and slashed across the face. May eventually have bled to death, but he thinks death was caused by the blows to the head, the kick and from hitting the concrete bench leg. Nothing different from what he told me. I wonder why the overkill?"

Another report seemed to interest Kalinski. "Here's the list of customers at that pub, Checkers. And we have a name!"

"Great. Who is it?"

"One Kyle Quigley, the puppy who kept following the girl around."

"Let's go over to that pub and see how long he was there."

At the pub, which was a block up the street from the Hillside Mall, the proprietor remembered the Quigley youth. "He's a regular here these days. Comes in when he gets off work at the supermarket in the mall. Mopes around a while."

"Is he old enough?"

"Yeah, I checked his ID card. He doesn't have a driver's license. He's eighteen, getting on toward nineteen. Don't worry. I do check on young guys who come in here."

The barmaid added her comments. "He's been coming in here and sitting around doing nothing ever since he got fired at Packard Electronics. He didn't think it was fair, and he doesn't make as much money at the supermarket. He's only a box boy."

"When did he come in Wednesday night?"

"About eight, I think. He usually does. He gets off at the mall at seven." She laughed. "Told me all his troubles once. Thinks I'm his mother confessor."

"How long did he stay?"

"Quite a while I think. He was sort of nursing a beer. I don't think he has much money and I suppose he didn't want to be turned out for not buying anything."

"What about you?" Rankin asked the proprietor.

"Yeah, that's probably right. I wasn't paying any attention to him. But he was drinking later that night. He had at least two more, maybe more than that."

"What time was that?"

"He came up to the bar right after the hockey crowd left, when things had thinned out. About ten-thirty or a quarter of eleven. There's an arena opposite the mall and there was a game last night. It's only a recreational league, but a lot of people go to the games."

"When did he leave?"

"Late. Maybe closing time."

The barmaid nodded agreement, then asked, "Why the questions?"

"We are investigating the Packard girl's murder and are interested in anyone with any connection to the Packard family."

"Well, I don't think he could have done it. Too much of a wimp if you ask me. Really immature."

"In what way?"

She thought for a moment, then said, "He probably had to have his mother tie his shoes before he left home each morning." The proprietor snickered.

"Hey, I heard she was mad because they killed her brother to take his organs," the barmaid remarked. "Seemed like a sensible thing to me when that happened. He was going to die anyway."

"Do you agree with the euthanasia law?"

"Sure. Why can't someone who's in a lot of pain ask to be put out of his misery?"

"What do you think?" Rankin turned toward the proprietor, who thought for a moment before he answered.

"I don't know. I sort of agree with what she said, but then that Packard kid got killed and I kinda wondered. But what I really think about it is that if everyone used all the money and time and effort for medical research instead it would do a lot more good than holding protests and such. Rich people like the Packards have a lot of money, so they can do these things, but they ought to use it somewhere that would do more good."

"The Packard girl's petition campaign was done all with volunteers and she said publicly that any money she got from the lawsuit would go to the hospice."

"That so? I guess that's okay then."

From the pub, the detectives walked down to the mall, noting the arena on the other side of the street and the bus stop at the edge of the mall. Quigley had not come to work yet. He was only a part-time employee. They headed to Quigley's home, which was not far away.

It was a basement apartment in a large older house and was approached by outside stairs to a small space outside the door. Leaves had collected in the stairwell, which was not drained, leaving a slippery mess. The door was opened by a gray-haired woman wearing a full-length apron over a print dress of cheap material, and carpet slippers over stockings rolled down to the tops of the slippers. On seeing them, her careworn face, lined with wrinkles, froze into a passive but unwelcoming expression.

"Mrs. Quigley?"

The woman nodded.

"Is your son, Kyle, here?"

"He's gone to work." Her toneless voice mirrored her expression.

"He's not there yet. Where else might he have gone?"

She gave a minimal shrug.

"Okay, we'll wait until he comes to work to talk to him. Don't worry. We're not accusing him of anything wrong. We only think he might be able to give us some information."

The woman shut the door in their faces.

In the supermarket, the manager led them to his office, not wanting an employee to be questioned by the police in full view of the customers. He went personally to get Quigley and bring him to the office.

"What do you want? I haven't done nothing." The youth had a surly expression on his long, thin face. He wiped a lock of unruly light brown hair out of his eyes.

"Where were you on Wednesday night?"

"What's it to you?"

"Just answer the question."

"I was here."

"Only until seven. Where were you after that?"

"I had a burger at the Burger Bin, over there." He motioned across the mall.

"Then you went to the Checkers Pub, didn't you?"

"Yeah. So what?"

"How long did you stay there?"

"All night."

"You used to be friends with Dawn Packard, didn't you?"

"Oh, her! Rich girl. Thinks she owns the world. That kind think they can order everyone around. I worked for her dad. She worked there and thought she could order me around because her dad was the boss."

"You're not sorry that she was murdered?"

164

He hung his head and scuffed the floor with his shoe, a battered old Nike the officers noticed. "Well, yeah. That's too bad. I'm sorry for her family."

"Okay, you can go back to work."

CHAPTER THIRTY-ONE

Back at the office, they dug out the report from the phone company. The call that had lured Dawn from the house to go to the bus stop was made from a pay phone at the mall. "That figures," Kalinski commented. "The guy had to be close enough to the bus stop to get up there by the time the girl arrived. In fact, he waited in the bushes for her."

"Not necessarily. Someone else might have stood there to shelter from the rain while waiting for the bus."

"If he did, he missed the bus. The one that came along a little after ten was the last that night."

"Besides, he could have come a little after the girl got there. She wouldn't have been afraid of someone walking up the street wearing a raincoat on that night."

"Yeah. How about the crank calls?"

"They were made from a pay phone on the other side of town. Whoever did it would have to have known how that petition drive worked in order to lure the girl to the bus stop."

"That would include all the people she knew. I think she got everyone going on it."

"But not the doctors."

"I wouldn't be so sure about that. Their lawyers would have filled them in pretty completely."

Rankin leaned back in his chair. "Okay, let's look at motive, means and opportunity. We don't have to prove motive, but let's look at it anyway. It seems to me that those doctors and the stepmother had the best. The lawsuit against them was dropped when the plaintiff died."

"I don't see it that way, for those doctors anyway. Because the trial never was completed, they didn't get a chance to tell their side of the story. They've made statements to the press, but no one pays any attention to them. But everyone remembers the impression the Packard girl made with her pleas for her brother's life. I figure she actually won that case."

"You might be right. But the stepmother still hated her guts. Okay, let's talk about means. Anyone with two hands, one foot and a knife had the means. That doesn't get us anywhere. And whoever was that angry would have had the strength."

"You're saying it didn't have to be the body building boyfriend," Kalinski laughed. "I still like him as a suspect."

"So do I. Now opportunity. The only one we can totally cross off is the guy who's in Switzerland. But his e-mails had apparently stopped. I suppose he could have made a trip over here on the sly."

"We haven't checked his home to see whether he came back," Kalinski observed.

"Would he have let his folks know if his intent was to murder the girl?"

"Why would he all of a sudden decide to do that, when he was thousands of miles away?"

"She might have said something in one of her e-mails to him. You said that she had deleted all her outgoing e-mails, and only kept the ones she received from him."

"Yeah, that's right. She kept her computer pretty clean."

"Did she clear her delete file?"

"She'd cleaned it up also. There were only a few entries in it, all within a day or two of the time she was killed."

"Smart girl. Not leaving anything around that she might regret later. We'll know more about the e-mails from him when we interview the friends tomorrow. No need to contact the Swiss police just yet."

"Unless she got some e-mails that were only intended for her and deleted them as soon as she got them."

"And didn't tell the aunt. We'll have to think about that."

They reviewed the incoming reports silently for several minutes.

"Whoever did this had to know the bus schedules," Rankin pondered. "That probably lets out those doctors."

"No it doesn't. That bus goes on up to St. Luke's Hospital, where it turns around and comes back. That's the hospital where those doctors were working, so they may well have known the schedule."

"St. Luke's. That sounds like a Catholic hospital. You wouldn't think they'd allow euthanasia."

"It doesn't have to be Catholic. St. Luke was supposed to be a physician and lots of hospitals are named after him. I think St. Luke's is run by the city. It's the one the ambulances take people to. That's why Brian Wall ended up there," Kalinski explained.

"Learn something new every day! Anyway, we'd better not forget the aunt. She didn't sound too enthusiastic about the girl's petition campaign. Or she might have had some personal reason that we don't know about. And we don't know whether that phone call to her number had anything to do with the murder. We only have the aunt's say so. There could have been some entirely different reason the girl was at the bus stop, one only the aunt knew."

"I can't see her doing that really brutal murder, though. If she was going to kill, I think she'd be more sly about it. She had lots of opportunity, with the girl living in the house. And this was a planned attack. The raincoat. The knife."

"Okay, I agree. It's not likely but is still possible. But let's leave it for tonight. When we come in tomorrow morning, we may have a fresh perspective on it."

"Good. I told my mom that if I got through early enough I'd take the dog to the vet. The vet's office is open until six, so if I go now, I can get there in time." What Kalinski was reluctant to say to his partner was that the trip to the vet was to have the ancient dog put down. That old dog now crippled with arthritis to the extent that it could not get up without help, had been Stan's constant companion in his teen-age years, and he did not want to listen to any joking comments about the appropriateness of his wanting to do this unpleasant chore.

"And I'll go see my dad and get him working on our obscene caller," was Rankin's only response. "I didn't get a chance to go over there this morning."

CHAPTER THIRTY-TWO

When Rankin called his parents' home, it was his mother who answered. "Why don't you pick up Gloria and the both of you come over for dinner. I'll do some fried chicken. And I just made an apple pie. If you are as skinny as usual, you need to be fed. No criticism of the way Gloria feeds you. I know it's your work that gets in the way of eating three squares."

"Mom, I'm not skinny. I'm slender. I'm a good weight for my height and I want to stay that way."

"You've always been the one who needed to put on weight. Now don't give me any argument. Come on over."

"Yes, Mom," Al Rankin replied in a mock tone of meekness. He called his wife, and she readily accepted the invitation. "I love your mother's cooking," she enthused. "If it makes her happy, she can fatten me up as much as she wants."

After dinner, as Gloria helped her mother-in-law with the dishes, the two men adjourned to the living room. Gus lit a cigar. "I have the feeling you want to ask me to do something for you. How can this old warhorse contribute to the modern art of crime detection?"

"You're right about that Dad. You know I'm on this Packard case."

Gus nodded.

"We're trying to find the person who made at least two obscene calls to the girl who was murdered, within a few days of her murder. There may have been more, but the girl's aunt only knows of two. Those two calls were made from a payphone in your local mall."

"Only two calls from there?"

"Only two that we, and the phone company, know of. He may have made calls from another phone, like a cell phone."

"It was a man, then?"

"Yes. The aunt says so."

"And you'd like me to see if I can put my finger on any weirdoes who might have made those calls."

"That's about it."

"Could the aunt tell you the gist of those calls, or any words the guy used?"

"I asked her. She remembers, but I can tell that she is very reluctant to say what she heard. It's not the kind of language she's used to hearing, and she may not even be familiar with some of the words. I asked her to try to remember as much as she could, and to write it down. I thought she might be more frank about writing it than speaking it out loud. I'll pick up her answer when I see her tomorrow. She also told me she would try to remember the exact dates and times the calls came."

"I'll talk to several of the guys and see if they know of anyone with that sort of history, or ask around about anyone having expressed negative opinions about the girl. I take it she was the one behind this anti-euthanasia campaign."

"That's right. But the aunt doesn't seem to think the calls had anything to do with that campaign, or the lawsuit. You know about her suing the hospital, and also her stepmother, because they were the ones who authorized euthanasia of the stepbrother."

Gus nodded. "More about her sex life, you think?"

"Yeah. That's what the aunt said."

"Anything in it?"

"Probably not. She had sex with one boyfriend, but wasn't promiscuous."

"It would be unusual in this day and age for a girl not to have had sex."

"I think this guy might keep an eye out for any attractive young woman who gets in the news and calls on speculation. He wouldn't have any trouble finding out where to call. The Packards are pretty prominent people. He also wouldn't have any trouble finding out where the girl lived, so he's definitely a suspect."

"Well, I'll put the word out. I expect we'll be able to track the guy down."

"Thanks Dad. I thought you'd like to do a little sleuthing on the side."

"You're correct there, my boy."

Rankin changed the subject. "Does the name Quigley ring any bells with you?"

"Sure does. Small-time con artist, slippery as an eel. We had a hard time pinning anything on him, and I don't think he ever served time. But we made life uncomfortable enough for him that we think he left town and is probably now someone else's problem. Left a wife and baby behind."

"How long ago was this?"

"Fifteen years at least. Fifteen to twenty. Why?"

"We went to talk to an eighteen-year-old kid this afternoon and were met by a woman who gave the impression of being afraid of the police. We don't have any current record of either her or the kid being in trouble, so we wondered what would have caused the animosity."

"Could be that one. What did you want to see the kid about?"

"He used to work at Packard Electronics, and the boss's daughter was his immediate supervisor, which he resented."

"Ha! So he's a suspect, is he?"

"Along with several others."

"Let me know how you're getting along with that, son. I may be out of harness, but I like to know what's going on."

"I'll keep you informed, Dad."

CHAPTER THIRTY-THREE

Stan lifted the old dog out of the car and led it slowly up the walk to the door of the veterinary clinic. The dog wagged his tail as he entered the waiting room. The staff at the clinic loved this old dog and showered him with hugs every time he came in. He had no bad memories of trips to the vet.

"You must be Mrs. Kalinski's son," the receptionist said. "Take him on into the exam room."

"I brought a note from Mom saying that she agrees to have this dog put down. Since you don't know me, she thought she'd better do that."

"Oh, good. I'll put this in his record and you won't have to sign a form. Dr. Glenn will see you in a moment."

Stan had hardly taken a chair, the dog settling at his feet, when the door opened and a young woman of about thirty with dark hair pulled back and fastened with a clasp at the back of her neck and wearing a white coat over green surgical scrubs walked into the room. "Mr. Kalinski, I'm Dr. Glenn."

Momentarily lost for words, he stammered, "I was expecting an older man."

She laughed. "That catches a lot of people. Dr. Thomas Glenn is my uncle. I've been working for him for a year now, and he seems to trust me enough that he's gone on a three-month holiday to Arizona. I'm Dr. Susan Glenn." She held out a hand and Stan took it, noting the firm handshake.

"Glad to meet you."

"So the old fellow is getting to the point where he can't stand, is he. Mrs. Kalinski called and said he was getting so he no longer seems to be enjoying life, and we agreed that he should be put down."

"Right. This old guy helped me through my teen-age years. I hate to part with him, but I know it's the right thing to do." He bent down and lifted the old dog onto the table. The dog licked his hand and he ruffled the hair on its neck.

"It is the right thing to do. Don't feel guilty about it."

Stan only nodded. When the job was done and the dog carried away by a technician, Stan asked, "Dr. Glenn, could I have a few moments to talk to you about something?"

"Yes. This is my last appointment for the day. Come into my office. I'd offer you coffee, but any that is left this late in the day won't be fit to drink." After they were seated in the office, the vet asked, "Now, what can I help you with?"

"I'm with the police force and we are investigating the murder of the Packard girl, which seems possibly to have been motivated by her petition to have the euthanasia law repealed."

"Yes, I know."

"What is your opinion of euthanasia for humans?"

"I am definitely opposed."

"But you do it to dogs."

She leaned forward in her chair. "Let me explain to you what the difference is."

"Okay. Fire away."

"Humans differ from other animals in that we are capable of abstract thought. We recognize right and wrong, good and bad. We can apologize and we can forgive. Other animals are only concerned with survival for themselves and their species, whereas humans can understand that something we do here today can affect someone else on the other side of the world tomorrow. We are the only animals with that capability of abstract thought. We can make plans for the future. If we are sick, we can understand what can be done to make us better. We have hope for the future.

"A sick or injured animal that is in pain doesn't live from day to day. It lives from moment to moment. A veterinarian not only has the right to free the animal from its pain, but also the responsibility to do so. The last euthanasia I will ever do will be as hard to do as the first, especially if it is a pet I have been taking care of all its life. There is no way I will get 'hardened' as people often suggest.

"A person who euthanizes another human is going to feel guilt about having committed what in all cultures and religions is the worst of all sins, that of taking the life of another person. Or they will have the guilt thrust upon them by other people. In order to deal with this feeling of guilt, they have to push the guilt aside in some way. The vet, however, doesn't have to feel guilt and is left free to grieve right along with the animal's owners. Grieving is a normal way to deal with the heartbreak of death. Vets don't have to push things into their subconscious. Am I making sense?"

"Absolutely. You are saying that you can lead a normal life, without guilt, because you have done something good, but the person who does it to another human will spend the rest of their lives having to suppress a feeling of guilt."

"That is correct."

"I never thought of it that way. What if the person really wants to die?"

"How can you be sure of that? A person who is that desperate is not one who is thinking clearly."

"One person I talked to thinks that a lot more money should be spent on hospices."

"I would agree with that. Not necessarily hospice care. Palliative care can be done at home or in a nursing home."

"He also thought that doctors are afraid that if they give enough narcotics to control a person's pain it might get them into trouble."

"That is an attitude that needs to be corrected. When an animal, including human animals, is really in pain, giving them enough of a narcotic drug to control that pain is not going to make an addict of them."

"Do dogs and cats ever get addicted to drugs?"

"I suppose it's possible, but you have to remember that we are concerned with far shorter periods of time than physicians are. The main problem in vet medicine is one of recognizing when an animal is in chronic pain. The vet schools are addressing that problem pretty thoroughly these days."

"Animals can't tell you when they're hurting."

"Yes they can, but you have to know what to look for."

"Well, thanks a lot for taking the time to explain this to me." Stan rose to his feet. He had noticed that the young woman was not wearing a ring on her left hand. He asked, "How about going out to dinner with me?"

She smiled. "I'd love that."

After one last check on the hospitalized animals in her care, Susan Glenn dashed to her upstairs apartment to change from scrubs to a dark gray pantsuit and a fiery red blouse. Putting on a light jacket, she met Stan in the waiting room and as they stepped out into the night she locked the door to the clinic. The weather had turned mild, with only a light breeze, still warm after a sunny afternoon. "I know a good restaurant only three blocks up the street. It's a lovely evening. Why don't we walk?"

"Fine with me," Stan said, smiling down at her. Anything to prolong what seemed as if it could be a pleasant evening with an attractive young woman. A sickle moon was just setting, stars already sparkled in the clear sky and a light breeze rustled the fallen leaves from trees that lined the street. They walked slowly up the street, soaking up the ambience of the evening.

After their meal, they dawdled in the booth of the restaurant, reluctant for the evening to end. They told each other about their lives, their education, their hobbies and their passions, each compiling a wealth of information about the other. They walked slowly back to the clinic. Should he kiss her goodnight? Stan wondered. After all, this was a first date. She might think him too hasty if he did. But she lingered on the doorstep after unlocking the door, and he decided to risk a discreet kiss. She seemed pleased and bade him goodnight with a nice smile. As he returned to his car, he had a fleeting memory of Al Rankin saying, "You need to find a girl you can go to…"

CHAPTER THIRTY-FOUR

Saturday morning Stan Kalinski returned the dog's collar and leash to his mother. "Sorry I didn't get these back to you last night, Mom. You didn't tell me that there's a new vet at the clinic. I took her out to dinner."

His mom smiled. "I thought you might like her."

"Mom, you are always telling me I need to meet some nice young ladies. I think you set me up."

"It might have crossed my mind."

At their office, he and Rankin reviewed the case so far.

"Dad says he thinks he can find out who our obscene caller was. He still has lots of connections. Dr. Packard called and said she would have the list of dirty words and phrases the caller used ready for us to pick up this afternoon. She's out this morning, but we can go to Charles Packard's house after our session with the students. The priest at their church is coming to talk about funeral arrangements at one o'clock, but after that we can meet her there. So let's go over everything we've got so far and see what we have to do next and write up our reports."

"Anything more from the lab?"

"Not until we find a coat or shirt in dark blue so they can compare those fibers. And you know how long it takes to get the DNA evidence. Not that they picked up much of anything to run DNA on, except the blood, in case the attacker had the same blood group as the girl and we can get a DNA profile on him—or her."

"It's not a common blood group, so even if he did cut himself with his knife, we would probably have found some A or O blood," Kalinski reasoned.

"But it's not that rare. There are hundreds of people around here with type B blood, including her family members."

"Yeah, I guess so."

"Damn the rain. The guy who did all that to the girl should have left something around the place. If he did, it got washed away in that downpour. I mean, it took some effort to do all that stuff. I wonder why he had to try to kill her in so many different ways," Rankin asked.

"It doesn't make sense, does it?"

CHAPTER THIRTY-FIVE

Margo Cunningham greeted them at the door of a house not quite as opulent as the Hamilton home, but still suggesting that its owner had a well-paying job. Her daughter Lindsey greeted them shyly and informed them that several of her friends would be there in a few minutes. They were picking up the pizza on their way. Soon the house was swarming with eager teenagers. The pizzas disappeared with amazing rapidity, but Rankin and Kalinski managed to acquire two pieces each. Margo, who they learned had been a high school teacher, called the kids to attention. She supplied Kalinski with a card table on which to write, and the young people scattered themselves around the room on couches, chairs and cross-legged on the floor. There were an even dozen of them, more than Rankin had expected.

He started off by asking the ones who had been on Jon Smits' mailing list to identify themselves. All but one of those on the mailing list were present. Another girl spoke for the other youths. "We all want to help any way we can with finding the person who killed Dawn. I guess what you really want is a lot of background. Is that right?"

A boy who turned out to be the clown of the bunch wisecracked, "Nah. They think one of us did it." He got a few giggles and even more frowns from the others.

"Lenny. Be serious," one girl remarked. "This isn't anything to crack jokes about."

"Sorry."

They all turned their attention toward the detectives. Addressing the first girl who had spoken, Rankin said, "You are correct. Let's talk about your e-mail correspondence with Jon Smits first, then I'll open it up to all of you to add anything you think might be useful. Now, when was the last time any of you received an e-mail from Jon?"

"A week or so ago," Lindsey answered. "I don't remember the exact date."

"More than that," one boy said. "More like ten days."

"Yeah, that's right. More than a week," another put in.

Rankin told them, "Dawn got her last e-mail from him eight days before her death, which was three days ago. Does that sound right?" There were affirmative nods and comments. "Did anyone who was not on that mailing list get an e-mail from him?" The answer was negative.

"I thought it was odd that he didn't write for so long," a tall, thin young man wearing glasses remarked. "He usually sent us something every three or four days." The others agreed.

"How about Twitter?"

"Same thing, only more often." Again there was agreement.

"What did he say to you in his last e-mail?" Their answers agreed with what they had read on Dawn's laptop—

he was in Davos and planned to go skiing. Rankin changed the subject. "Let's talk about Dawn. Had you noticed anything different about her recently?"

"What time period are you talking about when you say 'recently'?" the tall thin young man, who was studying law, asked.

"Let's say within a week of her death."

"No. I didn't notice any change in that time, but since her brother's death and when she started this petition, she has become sort of angry."

There were comments from others agreeing with this assessment. One girl remarked, "She got a lot harder to get along with."

"But we still liked her," another girl asserted. There were nods of agreement.

"None of us wanted to kill her," the clown added, getting dirty looks from several others.

"What did you young people think of her petition?"

Lindsey answered, "I think most of us signed it. We were all kind of shocked by what happened to Dawn's brother."

"Yeah," said another. "Most of us helped her with the petition drive. She had a table in the mall, until Alex Hamilton came to help out and opened that office. We've all volunteered at one time or another."

"But some of us were getting a bit tired of it."

"But she thanked us for helping."

"Yeah, she did."

The discussion became generalized and Rankin sat back and let the young people go at it.

"I still think old people with cancer who are in a lot of pain should have a way out."

A red-headed, freckle-faced boy who had identified himself as Andrew, one of Smits' e-mail recipients, entered the discussion, "My dad is a family physician. He says people underestimate what doctors can do to control pain. He tries to make his patients who are dying as comfortable as possible and gives them the option of total pain control even if it kind of knocks them out, or lesser amounts so that they can remain mentally alert to do things and have friends and family, and also clergy, come to visit them. He says that can be as important to a dying person as pain control."

"I think that's what the hospice does."

"Yes, but there is a long waiting list to get into the hospice. We need more hospice spaces. And it costs money, so it has to be paid for some way. In the meantime, palliative care can be done at home or in the hospital. Dad has patients in all those places."

"But look at what was done with Dawn's brother. His organs were all donated and saved several people's lives.'

"Do you think it's okay to kill a person to harvest their organs?"

"Brrr! Harvest. What a way to refer to it. Like harvesting corn or wheat."

"Like growing people to harvest their organs," the clown said.

"Oh, shut up!"

"But you have to admit, it helped several people."

"Maybe, but I've been thinking of putting on my driver's license that I don't agree to having my organs donated. I'd think that maybe if I was in an accident and was unconscious, they'd bump me off to take my organs."

"I'd hate to have my lungs transplanted into some old fart with lung cancer from smoking like a chimney all his life."

The physician's son responded, "But people who are born with cystic fibrosis also need lung transplants. Wouldn't you want to do that?"

A serious looking girl who had not spoken so far said, "If only you give yourself over to Jesus, he will save you."

"Didn't do Dawn's brother much good."

"He was a sinner. Riding around on a motorcycle. Those motorcycle gangs are dangerous."

"Not all people who ride motorcycles belong to gangs. I know lots of people who ride bikes because it's fun."

Rankin nodded to Kalinski and they both rose to go, leaving the discussion going on heatedly behind them. They thanked Margo Cunningham and left. Outside the house, Kalinski remarked, "It's amazing that everyone we talk to seems to be more interested in this euthanasia question than they are in the girl's murder."

"Yeah. Interesting isn't it? I'd expect it to be the other way around."

CHAPTER THIRTY-SIX

It was close to two o'clock when they arrived at the Packard home. As they parked on the street in front of the house, they saw a tall, stately, silver-haired man, wearing a clerical collar, leaving. As he approached them, Rankin asked, "Reverend James?"

"Yes, I am. And you?"

Rankin introduced himself and Kalinski. "Can we have a word with you?"

"Of course."

"We're investigating the murder of Dawn Packard, and we wondered if you could give us some information on the Packard family."

"Whatever I can without betraying things that are confidential."

"Sometimes even those have to be discussed in a murder case. We often have to breech the confidentiality of doctors and bankers also, if what they can tell us is relevant to the murder."

The priest nodded.

"I gather that the Packards attend your church."

"Yes, they do, but not regularly. I have been here less than two years. My predecessor would have been able to tell you more."

"We understand that Packard and his wife met through your church and that they were regular members then."

"That was before my time, so I can't tell you much there."

"Has either of them come to you to talk about their marriage? Mrs. Packard has left her husband and is threatening divorce."

"They have not talked to me about that. I only heard about the divorce this afternoon. I really don't know the family that well. I didn't know the daughter at all."

"Was it after the son's death when you came?"

"Yes it was, but I have heard a great deal about it. The congregation is about equally split on whether they agree with what was done to that young man."

"I would think that a church would be totally opposed."

The priest smiled. "If you were talking to Father Manuel at the Catholic Church, that is the answer you would get. It is much easier for a person who is totally committed to one point of view than for someone like myself, and many of my parishioners, who can see both sides of the question. The Church, both locally and nationally, is studying the issue and has not come up with a firm opinion on the matter."

"You say you yourself are on the fence?"

"I don't think that 'on the fence' is the way I would express it. I know that there are positive aspects of both sides. I think it has to be assessed on the basis of the facts in each individual case. In many such questions, where people take sides, it is not a question of right versus wrong, it is a question of differing opinions over two right answers. One needs to decide which one takes precedence."

Kalinski asked, "Do you have an opinion on the Brian Wall case?"

James sighed. "I'm afraid not. It is a serious moral and ethical question."

"In what way?"

"Is it acceptable to take the life of one person in order to save the lives of others?"

"In the military, the answer would be yes."

"In war, many ethical questions differ from those we face in peacetime. Morals seem to be suspended in many situations. Just because war has been declared, is it morally right to kill anyone?"

"Then, with Brian Wall's case, the morally right answer would be not to kill him, even if there were other people who might benefit from his death."

James thought for a minute. "My gut feeling would be that to let him live out his life would be the best option."

"The surgeon who transplanted his organs had the opposite view. He saw, every day, the suffering of people who needed donor organs."

"And I can appreciate his view. That is why it is a dilemma. And I know of one other case in which this issue came up. The grandson of one of my parishioners was an athlete, a gymnast I believe. He suffered a broken neck as a result of a fall and was paralyzed from the neck down. He could not reconcile himself to living in a wheelchair and not being able to do anything himself, according to his grandmother. She says that he referred to his paralyzed body as a prison. He opted for euthanasia, and donated his organs for transplant. He had to persuade his parents, and made them sign a pledge that they would allow his organs to be donated. In that case, good came out of his decision, though I thought that with proper counseling, he might have made something useful and satisfying out of his life. However, I did not know this individual, so I could not really express my opinion to his family."

"That's interesting," Kalinski remarked. "I didn't know there was another case like that. Was it local?"

"Yes."

Kalinski had a vision of Mrs. Mendel supporting her husband and saying that the Brian Wall case was a one-off. He remembered Dr. Mendel staring at the floor and not correcting his wife. "I wonder how often that is likely to happen."

CHAPTER THIRTY-SEVEN

Madge Packard handed over her list of words and expressions used by the obscene caller, blushing as she did so. Rankin assured her that, though it must have been repugnant to her, it would be useful to them.

"I know. I told myself that it was an academic exercise. That was the only way I could make myself write down some of those things."

As they left the Packard house, Rankin said, "I'll take this over to Dad. While I do that, you can put someone onto getting in touch with the police in Switzerland about the Smits kid. It's probably the middle of the night over there, but see what you can do. Then check with forensics about that poison pen letter."

Rankin drove over to his parents' house with Madge Packard's list. Gus took one look at it, shoved it away at arm's length with one hand and playfully fanned his face with his other. "We don't use dem words in dis house!" he exclaimed,

"Let me see," his wife demanded. "Oh my! We don't, do we?"

"Dad, you're having the time of your life, aren't you," Rankin remarked, laughing.

"You betcha! I'm just a dirty old man. Seriously, I'll turn this over to Dick Eames. He'll be able to find someone who knows someone who heard someone say something. You know how these things work. I can probably have an answer for you tomorrow."

"Thanks Dad."

While he waited for the call to Davos to be put through, Kalinski phoned the forensic lab. "Do you have anything on that poison pen letter we gave you?"

"I think there's a report here ready to go out. Do you want me to read it to you?"

"If you could, it would be appreciated."

"It doesn't amount to much. It was typed on an ordinary PC, not a Mac, of which there are thousands in this city. It was printed on ordinary computer paper and put in a standard envelope you can get at any office supply store. The person who sent it seems to know about DNA. It was only handled by the two ladies who received it. Thanks for sending us their prints. I hope they didn't give you any trouble about having their prints taken."

"No. The officer who went to take the prints says the girl's aunt was very gracious about it, and the other one was our corpse."

"Good. Anyway, no other prints on either the envelopes or the letter. It was sealed up by someone who knew that we can get DNA from saliva, so didn't lick the envelope. Used water to spread on the flap. The stamp was one of those that come ready to stick on without moistening. Everything was done while wearing gloves."

"Do you have any opinion on the contents?"

"The person was well educated in that the grammar and spelling and the punctuation were correct. It wasn't the usual poison pen letter. It was about this euthanasia debate, saying no one had the right to deny a person the kind of death they wanted and saying that someday the recipient would change her mind. The wording was more mean spirited than what I'm giving you. There was a veiled threat to the effect that the recipient, named Dawn, had better look out for her health, that accidents could happen."

"One did! I wonder…"

"I think you'll have to see if anyone close to her has expressed those opinions. This is a very personal letter, according to the technician who studied it. Either the writer knew this Dawn person, or knew all about her plans."

"Does it refer to things that the writer could have gotten out of newspaper articles or TV newscasts?"

"Possibly so."

"So not necessarily a family member or close friend."

"No. I guess not."

"Thanks a lot. I suppose a copy of it will be along with the report. We didn't read it because we didn't want to handle it except to put in an evidence envelope."

"Of course. You'll get a copy."

"Thanks."

When Rankin returned, Kalinski gave him the gist of what he had learned. "Doesn't sound as if it's from the same person who made the calls," Rankin observed.

"No, it doesn't, but I wonder if it could be one of those two men who wrote letters to the editor of the paper. When we get the copy of the report, let's see if there are any similarities."

"Why would someone send an anonymous letter if he could vent his spleen in the paper? But I suppose you're right. We should check." He stretched. "But let's call it a day. Those guys can wait. They're not going anywhere."

CHAPTER THIRTY-EIGHT

Dick Eames, the officer who was looking into the obscene phone calls, called on Sunday morning, soon after Rankin and Kalinski arrived in their office. "About that guy who made the obscene phone calls, we have a possible. A guy I know who hangs out in the West Hills Mall has heard an old man talking about young girls who get their pictures in the paper or on TV. Let's say he disapproves of them and does so in colorful language, some of which is the same as on your list. He thinks young women should stay at home, get married and raise kids. Same old stuff. But he seems to have it in for the ones who don't. Seems to think all of them are whores and are corrupting the morals of young men, who he doesn't think much of either, calling them wimps or pimps or something. My informant says the guy is senile and doesn't make much sense, but he hates girls who get themselves in the news.

"We managed to get a name for this guy. Oscar Lemon. He's known by a number of people who see him in the mall.

He apparently lives alone in a small house in the old part of town. Do you want to go with us when we go out to talk to him?"

"I don't think we need to. You can probably determine whether he might have something to do with the murder, or whether he's just an old geezer who wants to sound off. If you think he might be connected to our case, we'll come over, but right now, I'm waiting for an important phone call from Switzerland. Thanks Dick."

The call from Switzerland came late in the morning. To Rankin's relief, the speaker used perfect English, though with a hint of a German accent. Rankin hated trying to understand imperfect English spoken in foreign accents. He did not speak any other languages himself.

"We have located your young man, Mr. Jonathan Smits. He has, as he told his friends, been skiing. There is a lodge in the mountains where they have been staying for over a week. One must take a bus to the end of the road, then ski to the lodge. He was with several other young people he met at a hostel here in Davos. Since they must ski to the lodge, they took a minimum of supplies with them, only what they could comfortably carry in a backpack. The remainder of their possessions, they left in a secure storage locker here in Davos. They took their cell phones with them, but service in that area is very poor because of the mountains, so Mr. Smits was not able to send tweets to his friends. They only returned this morning. We met them as they got off the bus and informed Mr. Smits that you were concerned about his whereabouts. We did not tell him why, thinking that you might want to be the one to do so, but we went with him to retrieve his belongings from the locker. In our presence, he took out his computer and opened his e-mails. He seemed genuinely shocked at reading about the young woman's murder. He sent off responses to friends and family and is now trying to get a flight back home. I don't see any reason why we should not let him do so."

"No. We will be glad to have him back here. I assume that you verified that he actually spent all that time at this ski lodge," Rankin replied.

"We most assuredly did. He was there the whole time."

CHAPTER THIRTY-NINE

Eames took a uniformed officer named Jones with him to Oscar Lemon's house. It had probably once been an attractive bungalow with roses on a trellis over the front gate, flowerbeds and window boxes. Now it looked forlorn, overgrown with weeds, the roses untrimmed and the gate sagging on its hinges. The front yard was filled with junk, ranging from old tires to rings from six-packs of beverages.

When the old man opened the door to their knock, a blast of hot air redolent of spoiled food, urine and other forms of decay hit the policemen in the face.

"Whatdaya want," the old man asked querulously. He was clad only in shorts and undershirt. The heating in the house must have been turned on full force.

"We want to talk to you," Eames stated calmly. The old man merely stood there in the doorway. "Inside," Eames added.

Oscar Lemon turned silently and led them through the living room, which was choked with junk, into the kitchen.

As they followed him into the house, Jones commented quietly to Eames, "We should have requisitioned gas masks."

There was no place to sit, as Lemon plopped himself down on the only chair, breathing heavily through his mouth. He coughed, a deep rattling sound, and stared at the policemen.

"We want to talk to you about some phone calls you have been making."

"I don't have a phone. The damned phone company shut it off."

"From the mall."

"Half of them don't work."

"The calls I'm talking about were to a young woman named Dawn Packard."

"I don't remember the names of the girls I call. They're all trash. Whores. Running around getting into trouble, corrupting the men they prey on. They should be ashamed and I call them up to tell them so and tell them to repent before they do any more harm."

"How many girls have you called?"

"Lots of them. Loose ones. Shouldn't be out. Parents should be more careful what they let their daughters do."

"Look. Let's go down to the station and talk about this." Eames wanted to get out of the hot, smelly house before he passed out.

"I'll talk to you about those girls anywhere you want. We could go over to the mall and talk. I like it there."

"No. We'll go to the station. Put on some clothes. And why don't you turn down the heat while you're out of the house?"

"No way. They keep after you about wasting electricity. It's none of their business. I keep it on all the time because I don't like being told what I can do."

"Just put your clothes on and let's go." And hurry before I pass out, Eames thought. Lemon rummaged around until he found a pair of sweat pants and an old faded navy blue sweatshirt.

"Aren't you going to lock the door?" Jones called out as the old man hustled down the walk.

"Can't. The lock's broke and I can't afford what that locksmith said it would cost to fix it."

If you turned down the heat, what you saved on electricity would pay for a new lock, Eames reasoned.

At the police station, Eames could get nothing more out of Oscar Lemon than a runaround about the evil ways of the young women of this world. He called Rankin back.

"I don't think this is your bird. He doesn't seem to know anything about the murder, or associate the name Dawn Packard with anything that concerns him. I think he's just a dirty old man who wants to let girls he thinks of as lacking in morals know that he's on to them and that they will get into trouble if they don't mend their ways. The Packard girl is apparently only one of them. He's also a sick old man. I had Jones take him over to the hospital, and we're notifying Social Services."

"Well, there's another one off the list."

Kalinski suggested, "There's still the letter writer. We should get forensics onto comparing that letter with the ones written to the newspaper. They will be on the paper's website."

"Yeah. Let's do that tomorrow. Today I'd like to get re-acquainted with my wife. She hasn't seen much of me lately."

CHAPTER FORTY

When Stan Kalinski had an evening off, he usually cooked himself a full meal. His mother had taught all her children to cook, thinking that even the boys would have times in their lives when such knowledge would come in handy. Stan enjoyed cooking up some of the things he had liked so well when he was a child. However, on this night, he had something on his mind that he wanted to spend some time on, so he merely pulled a hungry-man frozen TV dinner out of the freezer and popped it in the microwave. He hardly tasted it as his mind was working on his problem while he ate.

For several days he had had occasional brief thoughts that he knew something that would have a bearing on the case. He thought that something someone had said had triggered these fleeting memories.

His mind flitted briefly to the rainy morning watching the police doctor examine the body. What had he said? Something about the person who had killed the girl being really angry. Nothing relating to this thought came to mind, so he abandoned it.

He decided to think about each of their suspects in turn. Reviewing what Al Rankin had told him about Clarice Packard, nothing of interest came to mind.

What about the doctors? Schumacher. What had Susan Glenn said about the attitude of a physician who had participated in euthanasia? He would become hardened, she had said, and would try to bury his feelings of guilt. Martin Schumacher was the prime example of that. He denied nearly everything, and tried to bolster his self-confidence by pretending to be the great surgeon whose patients couldn't do without him. But that didn't seem to have any bearing on this case.

Mendel. He hadn't corrected his wife's statement, but so what? Under the circumstances, it was the logical thing to do. And Stan still felt empathy toward the young surgeon.

What else had someone said?

He kept coming back to the comments about anger. What was it Rankin said just recently? Something about why the killer had tried to kill the girl in several different ways. That was it!

Stan rinsed out the tray his meal had come on and dropped the tray into the recycle bin. He went from his tiny kitchen to the living room area of his simple bachelor apartment, turning the chair at his computer desk around to face the opposite wall, which was lined with bookcases. For about five minutes, he stared at the books, then rose and went confidently to the middle section, taking a book from one of the shelves. He flipped it open and scanned it briefly. Yes, this was the one he wanted.

It took a little longer to find the chapter he wanted to read. When he found it, he sat at his desk and studied the material. Eventually he rose, a smile on his face, closed the book and put it back.

Now he knew who had murdered the girl.

CHAPTER FORTY-ONE

Rankin was already in the office when Kalinski sailed in the next morning, snapping his fingers and smiling broadly. "You're pretty happy this morning. What gives?"

"I think I know who did it."

"Well! I'm glad to hear that. What has the super-sleuth come up with?"

Kalinski leaned against his desk and grinned at his partner. "Every time you commented on how the killer attacked that girl in several different ways, I've had the feeling that there is something I ought to remember. So last night I sat down and stared at my bookcase. I thought it must be something I had read. After a bit, I got up and went over to the bookcase and pulled out a book. It was the one I was trying to remember. It had an account of a man who had been regarded in the latter part of the twentieth century as the world's leading forensic psychologist and criminal profiler, though he's undoubtedly dead by now. He had interviewed several famous serial killers, as well as a lot of others. And he devised a list of types of sex killers with descriptions of each."

"This wasn't a sex killing," Rankin reminded him.

"The sex isn't necessarily in the killing, but in the relationship."

"Okay. Go on."

"The one I was looking for was what he called the anger-retaliatory killer. He's an underachiever who finds power in manipulating someone by constantly making them do something for him. When she has had enough, and breaks off the relationship, he can't stand the loss of power. She's done him wrong, and that makes him feel he has the right to kill her. He stalks her and then when he decides to move in, his anger is such that he has to kill her in more than one way, ways that always include something like beating or stabbing. He doesn't want her to die right away. She has to suffer. And last, but not least, this type of killer always covers the eyes of the victim before he leaves."

Rankin stared at his partner for a long moment, then said softly, "Quigley."

"Yeah. Him. Kyle Quigley, who got brushed off by Dawn Packard after thinking he had a good thing going with her, who stalked her at her petition office and at her house, and who killed her with stabbing, punching and kicking as well as choking her. Then he dropped the raincoat he'd worn for protection over her face and walked away."

"You think he was capable of all that violence?"

"You heard what the police doctor said; when someone is that angry they can be pretty strong."

"Even a karate chop?"

"Remember Brewster telling us about the phys ed teacher who taught all the boys karate?"

"Okay. Let's go down to that pub and see if we can smash that kid's alibi."

CHAPTER FORTY-TWO

The pub was not open yet, but the proprietor opened the door for them and offered coffee when they turned down the offer of beer. The barmaid who had been working on Wednesday night was due to come on duty and was often a bit early, so to pass the time Rankin asked questions about the neighborhood, the local hockey team and the makeup of the patrons who frequented the pub. The man knew many of his regular patrons and said the hockey players and fans came in a group after games, to re-hash the scoring and either exalt or anguish over the result. He did not know most of these by name.

"There's a bell that tinkles when the door is opened and unless I'm really busy, I look up to see who's coming in or going home. I like to know, in case one of the guys who's a problem comes in and I need to watch him. And I like to get the feel of the hockey crowd. If they've won, they will be rambunctious, but they won't get into fights. If they've lost and someone starts needling them, it can break out into a fight."

"How was the crowd Wednesday night?"

"I could tell at a glance that the locals won. There were a whole bunch of them, and they were whooping it up."

"What time did they come in?"

"About ten fifteen, ten thirty. That's usually when the game is over."

The barmaid arrived and was asked to join the discussion.

"Now, let's get back to this Kyle Quigley kid who was here Wednesday night," Rankin started the questions. "How sure are you that he was here all night?"

The barmaid responded, "I've been thinking about that. He was sitting at that table over in the corner and nursing a beer. After he'd been there for a while, I went over. I'd been kinda watching him. I knew we were gonna be busy once the game got out and if he wasn't buying anything I was gonna suggest that he'd better do so. I tried to talk him into letting me get him another. He said he'd buy another in a few minutes, but not right then, so I left him alone."

"What was he wearing?"

"Gosh, I don't remember. Something dark like everyone wears these days."

"You can probably do better than that. Take your time."

"Okay. Let me think. Jeans. Maybe a black T-shirt, but he was wearing a coat all the time."

"A short jacket or a longer coat?"

"Longer, with patch pockets. Not real long. I'd still call it a jacket."

"Color?"

"Hmm. Dark, but not black. Navy blue maybe."

"What about his shoes?"

"I didn't notice them."

"Dark color?"

"Yeah, probably."

"Sneakers or runners? Or were they leather shoes?"

"You've got me there. I just have the impression of him all in real dark colors. Why?"

Rankin didn't answer her question. "Was there any time that night when you noticed that he wasn't there?"

"I wouldn't have noticed. Things were pretty busy, especially after the hockey crowd came in."

Rankin turned to the proprietor. "How about you?"

"I don't remember for sure. I have a vague feeling that he was there, but I didn't particularly notice him. I know he was there when the hockey crowd started thinning out. I think he bought himself three more beers. But I didn't particularly notice his clothes."

"If he had left, would you have noticed?"

"Probably, if it wasn't when we were real busy."

"Is there another exit?"

"Yeah, down there at the end of the hallway where the johns are. It's a fire door, but I had to disconnect the fire alarm when I'm open because people were always stepping out there to have a smoke. They can't get back in that way once the door shuts after them."

"But they'd block the door open so they could get back in," the barmaid added. "Whenever I saw it blocked open, I'd yell at them to shut the damn door. Most of the customers were pretty good about it."

So if Quigley went out that way, Rankin thought, he could have been seen leaving the premises or coming back and throwing a knife in the bin if anyone was out there smoking. He might leave that way if no one was around, but he might have to come back in the front door. Had he planned on that?

"If someone went out that way and had to come back in the main door, would you have noticed?"

"If it was someone I knew, I might. If you're thinking of Quigley, I don't remember him doing that."

"Could he have come back in with the hockey crowd without your noticing it?"

"Oh, sure."

In the background, Kalinski heaved a sigh of relief. Quigley could have done it and his theory was still standing up to analysis. The hockey crowd started coming in about ten fifteen. The timing was right.

The detectives left by taking the corridor to the fire door. Rankin paused by a pay phone across from the men's room.

"Ha! Look at this." He pointed to the phone number. It was the one the phone company had given them for the call to Madge Packard's house. "I suppose our phone company could call this a phone at the mall. It's near enough. It would have helped, though, if they had said it was a phone in the Checkers Pub."

When they left, Kalinski commented, "One beer to settle his nerves before the act and three more to calm him down after he'd done it."

"Yeah. Let's go get a warrant to search that kid's clothes closet."

CHAPTER FORTY-THREE

At the Quigley home, Kyle's mother opened the door with the same defeated expression on her face that they had seen before.

"Is your son here?"

"He's at work."

"On days this week?"

She nodded, accepting the warrant silently, and letting them into the apartment. In Kyle's room, she watched with an anxious frown on her care-worn face. They placed a pair of high-topped dark brown shoes, well scuffed, into an evidence bag. The toe of the right-hand shoe had been wiped off, but stuck in the crack between the sole and the toe there remained a small amount of a sticky substance that could be blood, skin and hair. There were no dark colored jackets. Quigley had probably worn his jacket to work.

"I don't see any jeans here. We know he wears them."

"In the laundry." She led them to the kitchen, where a small stackable laundry pair had been fitted into a corner. She pointed to a hamper. Kalinski dug into it and at the bottom found two pairs of jeans. One was old and almost drained of color from numerous washings. The other was newer and darker. Near the bottom of the right leg there were several small spots of something dark. Didn't even have the common sense to throw the jeans in the wash when he came home that night. Left it to his mother to do, Kalinski thought. He placed both pairs in a bag and gave Mrs. Quigley a receipt.

They left the exhibits at the forensic lab and went back to the station to pick up a couple of uniformed officers. At the supermarket Rankin placed one at the front and the other at the back door.

Entering the supermarket, Kalinski apologized to the manager. "I'm sorry, sir. I'm afraid we are going to deprive you of the services of one of your box boys."

Spotting Kyle Quigley who was stocking a shelf with canned goods, they walked purposefully toward him. The youth saw the detectives coming, dropped the box holding the canned goods, which spilled across the aisle, and ran for the rear exit. Hindered by having to do some fancy footwork among the rolling cans, Rankin and Kalinski made for the exit. It led to a corridor to the back door, which was now swinging shut, as Quigley had gained valuable time. But as they reached the door, they could hear a scuffle outside. The cop on duty there had moved quickly to cut off the fleeing youth's escape. He was just applying handcuffs to Quigley's left wrist as the detectives approached. But the youth twisted expertly from the policeman's grasp and struck him a hard blow on the side of his neck, managing to wriggle out of the temporarily stunned cop's hold. He sprinted across the parking lot, the handcuff dangling from his left wrist.

"You okay?" Kalinski asked the cop.

"Yeah," he replied rubbing the side of his neck. "Sorry."

Rankin yelled into his radio, "Set up a cordon around the west side of the Hillside Mall area. And send the dog unit." To Kalinski, he said, "Let's go get the kid's jacket. The dog can get his scent off that."

The dog handler arrived with Radar, a German Shepherd. The dog sniffed the jacket and was turned loose in the parking lot. Within seconds he had found the scent and streaked off across the lot, weaving back and forth among the cars. At the end of the lot, the dog made off down an alley with the cops in hot pursuit. The trail took them along several streets and alleys, once across a large residential yard, where a woman who was raking leaves stared in amazement at the procession crossing her property. Finally the dog came to a stop at the side of Hill Street, a wide thoroughfare. The handler motioned him across the street, where after a quick sniff in each direction, he picked up the scent again. Sirens could be heard as police cars screamed toward the area.

Radar, the dog, stopped at a fence and looked to the handler for directions. There were a few fibers of the color of Quigley's T-shirt caught on the top of the fence. The cops found a gate and shoved it open. Radar streaked through and picked up the scent on the inside of the yard. It led to a shed, the door now shut. Radar crouched in front of the door, barking.

Policemen congregated in front of the shed. Rankin sent some to cover the sides and rear, then shoved the door open. Radar entered and stopped near the back, jumping skyward to direct his handler's attention to the rafters. The youth was up there, perched on some boards that had been stored on the overhead beams. He again used the same tactics to delay his capture, though common sense should have told him it was no use. He threw the boards down, one at a time. The dog danced around the falling timber, but the men held their ground, waiting for the youth to give up. His perch was getting ever more precarious, as he threw more of the boards on which he was perched down at the waiting cops. Finally he lost his balance and nearly fell, catching hold of the rafter in time to prevent a fall. But the dog handler saw his chance and leaped up to grab the dangling handcuffs, pulling enough to almost dislodge the youth from the beam. The dog stood below, snarling, his upper lip rolled back from his gleaming teeth.

"The dog won't hurt you if you come down quietly," the handler said in a calm voice. "If we have to pull you down, I can't guarantee anything."

"Go away. Get that dog out of here," was Quigley's defiant answer. He was shivering, possibly because of fear, but more likely from cold. He had run off with nothing more on the top part of his body than a T-shirt.

The handler jerked on the handcuff, nearly pulling the youth off the beam.

The defiance went out of Quigley. "Wait! I'll come down."

"Don't try to do anything tricky."

"Okay, but can you take that dog away?" Quigley whined.

"When you're down and handcuffed. Not until then." However, he motioned the dog back a ways and let go of the handcuff. Quigley rolled off the beam, holding onto it with both hands and let himself down to where he could drop onto the floor between a lawnmower and a snow blower. The handler moved in and grasped his right arm, pulling it toward the youth's back and applied the second cuff. Only then did he call off his dog and turn his captive over to Rankin.

As they led Quigley away, Kalinski watched the dog handler give Radar his treat and ruffle the hair on his neck, praising his work. Seeing Kalinski's interest, he said, "To Radar, this is just a game. He does it for treats. You always have to give the dog his reward after a successful capture."

"What if the person he's sent to find is a lost child. He'd scare the child silly."

"They understand the difference. Until we opened the shed door, Radar didn't know whether he needed to be aggressive or not. He judges from my commands, but also from the fact that this kid was aggressive toward us."

"Smart dog."

"Yeah," the handler grinned. "He is." He gave the dog another treat.

Kalinski was still holding Quigley's dark blue jacket. He walked to the nearest police car and asked for an evidence bag. The jacket would go to the lab to compare its fabric with the threads found on the inside of the raincoat that had been thrown over the girl's body.

CHAPTER FORTY-FOUR

At the station, Quigley's first remark was "I want a lawyer."

"Do you know one you want to call?"

"I don't know any lawyers."

"We'll get one for you."

They left Quigley in an interview room while they reached the public defender on call. When the lawyer arrived, he asked, "Has Quigley been advised of his rights?"

"He has. Once at the time and place of his capture, and since we were not sure he was paying attention at that time, again as soon as we brought him here."

Rankin and Kalinski went with the lawyer to the interview room. Rankin opened the questioning. "Kyle Quigley, you are being charged with the murder of Dawn Packard. Do you want to make a statement?"

"I didn't do it."

"Okay, we'll start from the beginning." He questioned Quigley about his work at Packard Electronics and his relationship with Dawn. Occasionally the lawyer intervened to caution Quigley not to answer a specific question. When the questioning got to the point of Quigley's movements on Wednesday evening, Rankin sat back and let Kalinski take over. As Kalinski outlined the way they thought Quigley had committed the murder, he watched the youth get progressively paler until he was afraid the youth might pass out. The defense attorney said nothing during this narrative.

"What do you have to say to that?" Rankin asked, and again the youth responded weakly that he hadn't done it. His denial did not hold much conviction, but he continued, as the questioning progressed, to deny involvement in the murder.

In mid-afternoon, an officer popped his head in the door and motioned to Rankin, who stepped out into the corridor. "Here's the preliminary report from the lab."

Rankin read it and smiled. He re-entered the interview room and sat down opposite Quigley, leaning forward and talking in a loud voice rife with accusation, shaking the report in the youth's face.

"Blood spots on the jeans you wore Wednesday night were of group B, an uncommon blood type, which is the type of the victim. Material taken from the right shoe of the pair you were wearing is composed of blood, also group B, skin and hair which compares with that of Dawn Packard. DNA will eventually confirm this. Fabric from your jacket matches that of fibers retrieved from the inside of the raincoat you wore when you attacked the girl."

The youth slumped over the table so hard his head banged on the surface. He lay there sobbing. The lawyer said, "May I have a few minutes alone with my client?" the policemen walked out of the room.

224

Several minutes later, the lawyer called them back in. "Mr. Quigley is prepared to make a statement."

Quigley's statement was much the same as the scenario the police had described. There was one slight change. He had planned to stab the girl many more times than he did, but was interrupted by the bus's early arrival. He had scurried into the bushes, giving the girl a slash across the face as he left her. He hastily removed the yellow raincoat in order not to be seen. He had planned to be finished before the bus was due and was afraid that it would stop. But it didn't, so he went back to drop the raincoat over her face, but she had given a rattling breath, causing him to realize that she wasn't dead yet, so he hauled off and kicked her in the head. As he heard the cracking sound her head made when it hit the leg of the bench, he thought it was the best sound he had ever heard.

When Kalinski heard him say this, it vanquished any lingering vestige of sympathy he might have had for the hapless youth.

They had been right about him going out the side door of the pub, Quigley said. He had blocked the latch with a piece of cardboard, but it had fallen out by the time he got back. Yes, he threw the knife and the towel it had been wrapped in, into the dumpster. He had been lucky to find the hockey crowd entering the pub and had joined with them to re-enter the building. When he had gone up to the bar to order another beer, he had deliberately gotten into a conversation with the proprietor in order to be remembered.

It was late afternoon and getting dark by the time Quigley's statement had been typed and he had signed it. Rankin asked him if he wanted to call his mother, but he hung his head and shook it. Thinking of the woman sitting at home wondering what was happening to her boy, he decided to call her.

"I was wondering what that boy had gotten into," she said, her voice sounding defeated.

Rankin told her, "You can come visit him if you want to. I'll tell the desk that it's okay."

"I think I will," she replied tentatively, and then very softly added, "Thank you."

Before he went back to his desk, Kalinski made a detour out to the parking lot where he could make a phone call in private. He called Susan Glenn. "We've just cracked our case and I feel like celebrating. How about going out to dinner?"

"Why don't you come here and have a casual dinner and you can tell me all about it. I can do up a paella, with some French bread and a bottle of wine. Come about seven."

"That sounds great! See you at seven."

Rankin was on the phone, calling first Charles Packard, then Dr. Madge. He asked Kalinski to phone the two doctors and Keith Wall, to tell them they were free to leave. After the calls had been made, Rankin remarked, "I like those Packards. They have always been cooperative and never complained that we hadn't caught the guy the instant the murder happened."

"Yeah. They have class. Not like Schumacher." Schumacher, when told, had replied in a grouchy voice, "Well, it's about time." He had hung up the phone before Kalinski could say anything more. On the other hand, when Mrs. Mendel had answered the phone, she had been grateful and had thanked him for his call. Keith Wall was also grateful, more because they had solved the crime than because he could now go home. He would stay for the funeral anyway.

"Did you call Clarice Packard?" Kalinski asked.

"Nah. Why bother. Let her wonder if she's still on the suspect list until she sees it on the news." Kalinski laughed and agreed.

"You know," Rankin remarked, "for all that hullabaloo over this euthanasia law, in the long run it came down to a plain ordinary garden-variety lovers' tiff."

The End

About the Author

Carolyn Dale is a pen name of mystery author Anne Barton.

Anne Barton is a retired veterinarian and flight instructor. In her retirement, she has taken up writing mystery novels. She has also written one autobiographical book and numerous articles and short stories. Her short story won the Bloody Words Crime Writers' Conference contest in 2001 and is published in Bloody Words, The Anthology.

Born in Drumheller, Alberta, she grew up in Northern Idaho, returned to Canada, and now lives in the beautiful Okanagan Valley in British Columbia, where she is deeply involved with Habitat for Humanity and her Anglican Church work – that is, when she isn't riding horses or curling.

www.annebartonmysteries.ca
www.mysterycarolyndale.ca